VAMPYR LEGION

ALAN GIBBONS

Orion
Children's Books

First published in Great Britain in 2000
as a Dolphin paperback
Reissued 2010
by Orion Children's Books
a division of the Orion Publishing Group Ltd
Orion House
5 Upper St Martin's Lane
London WC2H 9EA
An Hachette UK Company

3 5 7 9 10 8 6 4

The Orion Publishing Group's policy is to use papers that
are natural, renewable and recyclable products and made
from wood grown in sustainable forests. The logging and
manufacturing processes are expected to conform to the
environmentalregulations of the country of origin.

A catalogue record for this book is available from the British Library
Printed in Great Britain by Clays Ltd, St Ives plc

ISBN 978 1 85881 835 1

www.orionbooks.co.uk
www.alangibbons.com

*'We fight neither to win nor to lose,
but to keep something alive.'* T. S. Eliot

PROLOGUE

The Attack

They attacked an hour before dawn.

Daybreak or dusk, at the trembling crossroads between day and night, that's when they always came, the times when their enemies' defences were most likely to be down.

It was the way of the Legion.

Bird's Eye saw them first. It stands to reason. That was his way – to see. He was the boy with the sight. He didn't actually *see* them, of course. Not in the way most people think of seeing, the physical interaction of light, pupil, retina and optic nerve. His sight was so much more fine-tuned than that, a spirit thing. Mysterious too – a living, growing part of him, after all these years still surprising and new. That grey winter's morning the sight exploded into his brain like a dumdum bullet, the advance shadows of the Legion bursting into his half-awake mind and yanking him to his feet with all the force of an electric shock.

'Mother, Tom, Captain Lawrence, it's started. They're back!'

Images of the invaders were overloading his mind. The black flutter of the Legion's airborne troopers, the grey ghosting of the Wolvers. Sounds that filled his every waking moment, and many of his sleeping ones too. They used to come in small groups: twos, threes; fives or sixes at most. Now it was tens, dozens. He trembled to think what might lie in store.

A second shout to alert the others.

1

'They're here!'

Then the adults were scurrying round the room, shouting, crashing over the makeshift furniture, snatching up their weapons, taking over from the boy in that way adults do, but eternally grateful for his gift of sight. Bird's Eye was a boy who could see for miles. He saw every road and building and living thing, and much more besides.

'Tom, Ann, brace yourselves,' said Captain Lawrence as he loaded his revolver. 'This could be bloody. But win or lose, I aim to send a few of them off to Vampyr heaven.' At the bitter laughter of his comrades, he chose his words more carefully: 'Very well then, Vampyr hell.'

In his former life the tall, moustachioed adventurer had been a military man, a commissioned officer. Since the coming of the Legion, he'd become a Vampyr hunter, living outside the law and outside society, stalking the city's demons. His life hadn't always been like this. He had once had a dream of career and family. But the dream soon vanished, the way his own young family had vanished. That was the reason for his crusade. The Vampyr tornado had broken over his wife and three children. Nobody was safe. Worse still, the attacks were becoming ever more frequent.

'It's going to be all right, darling,' Ann told her son, at the same time loading a bolt into her crossbow. 'We've defended this position before.'

It was true. They had. Twice that night, in fact. But it was going to be different this time. The sight told Bird's Eye as much. There was nobody left to man the forward defences. Front line, rearguard: suddenly they were more or less the same thing. Just small knots of fighters pulled back into the corridors of the labyrinthine building, ready to fight the final desperate action. Their beleaguered band had suffered terrible losses. Losses! Bird's Eye told himself he would never forget what that word really meant, the people who'd gone down fighting.

Heroes.

2

'Here they come,' said Tom Beresford, his cheeks puffing with fright. He'd once been stationmaster on the Great Western Railway, a pencil-thin beanpole of a man, armed with a home-made crossbow and a length of lead piping. Despite all Ann's pleading, he'd insisted she keep her pistol. Bird's Eye didn't exactly know why he did that, why Tom was prepared to put her life ahead of his own, but there was no time for questions. Seeing Tom gripping the lead pipe in his bony fist made Bird's Eye shudder. He knew that if it came to hand-to-hand fighting they were already dead. Their enemy was as strong as steel. As unfeeling too.

'Our chaps have opened up,' said Captain Lawrence. 'Hear them?'

Bird's Eye listened to the snap and zing of their bullets. But the snipers crouching by the sash windows of the old mansion house couldn't prevent the familiar thump, thump, thump of clawed feet landing on the roof. There had to be a dozen of them. It was round one to the Legion. This time there were too many Vampyrs to hold off with sniper fire alone. After that they heard the frenzied scratching at the outer doors. The Wolvers had arrived, claws penetrating the oak panels like diamond-tipped drills. Both units of the enemy commando were engaged. When it was time to storm the defensive positions, it would be the Wolvers first. They were the advance guard, the moon-born, the rippers. They were used to storm the enemy lines. Then it would be the turn of the elite fighters, the Vampyrs themselves.

If I have to fall here, Bird's Eye thought, I want the Wolvers to take me. It will be savage, and it will be bloody, but at least it will be over in seconds. It was different with the Vampyrs. They bit, they drank. If you were lucky, you died there and then. Otherwise, you faded slowly with the fever. What some called *the contagion*. It could take days to die, possibly even weeks, but by the end you were begging for it to be over.

The contagion left you as mad as a sewer rat and desperate

for death. Bird's Eye had seen its victims, creatures so ravaged with pain they looked like translucent ghosts on their beds. Most unspeakably of all, some of the Legion's victims had themselves been transformed into warriors of the undead, servants of the Legion.

'Destroy them,' said Tom, talking to the defenders beyond the walls. 'Obliterate them all.' He gave an uneasy smile. 'When I was reading about Vampyrs and Wolvers as a boy, I never thought I'd have to face them in the flesh. I thought they were just stories then, you know, like the Bogey Man. Never for a moment did I expect to see them for real. Leastways, not in this world.'

'Nobody did,' said Captain Lawrence. 'If I'd been asked to place a bet on how the world would end, I wouldn't have put my money on the contents of a lurid Penny Dreadful.' He broke off abruptly, unable to speak over the gut-wrenching sound of men begging for their lives, then their pitiful screams as the Wolvers did their work. No more sniper fire. The Legion was mopping up on the upper floors.

'They're inside the building,' murmured Captain Lawrence, 'Let us pray that our defences hold.' Bird's Eye exchanged glances with his mother. She'd made a determined move for the door.

'I should be up there,' she said. 'I don't want anybody fighting my battles for me. I've got to face them. It's my destiny.'

'Forget it, Ann,' said Captain Lawrence, cutting her short, 'You and young Robert are all that's left of the Van Helsing line. Your survival is our number one priority.'

But why is my family so important, wondered Bird's Eye. What had he missed while he was away at boarding school?

Lawrence pre-empted Ann's protests with a raised palm. 'No Ann, that's my final word.' And so it was. They had no choice but to stay there, holed up in their dank cellar.

Bird's Eye took in the shabby walls and he could feel the pressure of the Legion's attack. He was shut away, hoping to live but expecting to die, and horror was sealed inside that awful place with him.

Captain Lawrence was still reminding Ann Van Helsing of her importance. 'Your survival is our number one priority. Please don't argue the point any further.'

Ann nodded, and Bird's Eye watched her as if she was made anew. She was more than just his mother. She was Ann Van Helsing, Vampyr hunter, prophet of doom, and she'd seen this catastrophe coming. Unbeknown to her son, she'd been part of the Committee of Nine all along. Only in the last few weeks had young Robert, Bird's Eye to the Vampyr-hunters, gradually begun to understand just who she was, and what his grandfather had been before her. Now, as far as anyone knew, Ann was one of the Committee's two surviving members. The other seven were lying slain in their graves, or missing, presumed dead.

'Oh my,' said Tom, flinching at the dull thunder from above, 'Will you listen to that?' The corridors of the middle floors were echoing with a furious volley of rifle shot.

'Hold them,' said Captain Lawrence, urging his comrades on. 'Just keep them off for another hour, hold on until daybreak. You can manage one brief hour, can't you?'

It was during those agonizing minutes, when the battle was still hanging in the balance, that Bird's Eye got the sight again. Somebody was watching him. He turned his head to the left then to the right, as if expecting to discover a hole in the wall, and, pressed to it, a peeping eye.

'What is it, Bird's Eye?' asked Tom. 'Another premonition?'

Bird's Eye nodded slowly. There was someone, a shadow, there was . . . *him*.

Somebody faded and blurred, like an unwanted intruder in a wedding photograph, brushed out to save the blushes of the guests. He was standing at the end of a lonely parapet, atop a mist-wreathed castle. About him there rose a symphony made of Wolvers' howls and the shriek of hundreds of glossy black ravens.

'The lair of the Beast,' murmured Bird's Eye. Noticing everyone staring, he blushed. But nobody made fun of him. There had been a time when people had scoffed at the sight, but it was proving too useful too often. He'd earned the trust of the entire band.

'What's wrong?'

'I don't know,' Bird's Eye admitted. 'But I've got the strangest feeling that we're being watched.'

It was true – they were. But not by the Legion, and not by hidden spectators either. The eyes that watched them were looking on from a realm of darkness more complete than the blackest night. They belonged to the architect of the demon invasion. It was a hopeless game Bird's Eye and his comrades were playing. They were predestined to lose, predestined by *him*.

'Try keeping it to yourself, my boy,' Captain Lawrence advised. 'You keep talking that way and you're going to have every man Jack of us spooked.'

Bird's Eye nodded, but the feeling didn't leave him. He was being watched all right. The curious thing was, he had a notion he'd get to meet the watcher one day. More than a notion, *a knowledge*.

'The firing's coming closer,' said Tom, combing back his thin blond hair with the fingers of one raw-boned hand. Bird's Eye found himself staring at Tom's other hand. It was shaking. 'I know lad, I'm scared. I don't mind admitting it.'

'We're all scared,' said Ann. 'Every single one of us. There's no shame in fear. Not when there's something to be afraid of.'

Overhead, the interval between shots was getting longer. They all knew what that meant. The Legion was closing in. Soon they were able to make out the spit and clatter of crossbow bolts. Now it was bow against fang and claw.

'Do you hear that?' said Ann.

'This is bad,' said Tom, approaching the door and inspecting the dents made by the Wolvers' claws. 'Really bad.'

'Get to your places everyone,' said Captain Lawrence, seeing the splintered wooden panelling. 'Something tells me we're going to have company sooner than expected.'

The corridors overhead echoed with screams, and the noise of running feet. The next sounds that could be heard came from the approaches to the cellar. *Their* level. The wolf was at the door. The terror was approaching. Soon it would crash over them like a hurricane. Captain Lawrence held the revolver in a two-handed grip. Tom hung on to his crossbow and tucked the lead pipe in his waistcoat.

Ann drew her gun. 'We're going to hold them off,' she said. 'You see if we don't.'

Tom tried a smile, but it just wouldn't take on his ashen face. His jaw was frozen into a tight grimace. Fear had him by the throat and the shakes were so bad he could hardly stand. His legs had turned to water.

'What did I tell you?' Captain Lawrence barked, feeling the sense of resignation all around him. 'To your posts, everyone. What is it with all of you? Do you really want to feel those suckers gnawing at your necks? Of course you don't; you want to live just as much as I do.'

It was the sort of speech he had given on the battlefields of two colonial campaigns, but never had the enemy been so cold, so ruthless, so elemental. Never had the words sounded so false. 'Well, just hold on to that,' Lawrence continued, going through the motions. 'You want to live, don't you dare surrender. Don't you ever give up.' He stormed up to Tom, as if warning him that when it came to being scary a Wolver had nothing on Captain James Lawrence. 'Do I make myself clear? Nobody here is going to simply lie down and die. Not while I've still got breath in my body.'

Bird's Eye and Ann climbed on to a wooden barrel. This was the escape route, if all else failed. It was pushed against the wall, giving access to a coal hatch. A woman or a child might just be able to squeeze through. There was no hope for a full-grown man. Ann and Bird's Eye were reluctant to use it. It would mean abandoning their comrades.

'This is it,' said Tom hoarsely as the corridors fell silent. 'The defences are down.' A tear spilled from his eyes. His son Harry had been out there. 'We're all that's left.'

There was a long silence.

'Come on, you infernal fiends,' growled Tom, shouldering the crossbow. 'You have taken my boy, my only son. I've nothing left to live for now. Only revenge. What are you waiting for? Do it.'

The seconds ticked away. Captain Lawrence shifted his feet, taking his weight first on the left then on the right. 'Is it over?' he murmured.

Ann glanced at Bird's Eye. He shook his head. 'I see blood.'

'Get ready,' Ann ordered.

The door crashed open with a thunderclap, then the Wolvers were spilling snarling into the cramped, candle-lit cellar. They were killing machines, their huge shoulders built to act as battering rams, their man-trap jaws capable of breaching walls. The Vampyrs followed, hissing and screeching. The room resounded with hellish battle-cries. In such an enclosed space, the noise was unbearable.

Captain Lawrence opened up, bringing down two Wolvers with fast, accurate shots. A third was moving behind him, but Ann shot it and moved to finish it off with mallet and stake. Tom slew one of the Vampyrs with his crossbow, the bolt's impact spinning it round on its heels, a hideous scream catapulting from its throat. But the Legion was attacking in force and they were overrunning the hunters' positions, penetrating the defensive lines with their ferocious speed. Captain Lawrence was the first to fall, knocked off his feet by the impact of a Wolver's pounce.

A pair of Vampyrs joined the Wolver.

Bird's Eye yelled inside himself. *Get off him. Get off!* But no sound came. All he could see were Captain Lawrence's legs kicking wildly as he tried to tear the suckers from his throat.

'Hang on, James,' cried Tom, advancing and firing the bow into the chest of the closest Vampyr. But before he could reload a Wolver detached itself from the group around Captain Lawrence and sprang. In a grey snowstorm of snapping and tearing it was over. The bow and the lead pipe clattered across the floor.

No! The silent scream jolted hard inside Bird's Eye. 'Mother, we've got to do something.'

She nodded and ran forward, grabbing the lead pipe and locking it over the throat of one attacking Vampyr. She wrestled with the sucker for a few moments than slapped a stick of dynamite into Captain Lawrence's palm.

He managed an anguished smile then waved her away. 'Don't hang around on my account. I'm bitten, Ann. Finished. Just get out of here.'

Another Vampyr drew its thin, almost colourless lips back and steadied itself, ready to make a strike at Ann and add her to the Legion's long list of victims. But she was alert to the danger, pumping a shot into it at close range, then dispatching the fallen ghoul with a stake.

'Let's go,' she cried, shoving Bird's Eye towards the hatch with all her strength as the Legion gathered for the final assault: the move that would give them their main prize – Ann.

'But what about Captain Lawrence?'

'There's no way back for him now,' said Ann. 'But he's going to leave this world the way a soldier should. He knows what to do.'

As Bird's Eye followed her into the darkness of the over-grown garden, the last thing he saw was Captain Lawrence lighting the fuse on the dynamite. Then they were racing through needle-sharp thorn bushes and stumbling over criss-crossed tree roots. Ann cursed her long skirts.

Bird's Eye could still feel the eyes of the watcher on him. He was still thinking about him when the dynamite went off, whip-cracking across the cellar and belching fire, smoke and murderous shards of glass into the garden. The bushes behind the backs of mother and son were shredded by a hail of glass and debris. Bird's Eye wanted to testify out loud, to say goodbye to Tom and Captain Lawrence and hear the words ringing out across the sleeping city. But the words never came.

That was the moment they burst through the foliage and onto the mist-dampened pavement. They were on a poorly lit street in west London.

'Don't look back, Robert,' said Ann, hitching up her skirts. 'Just keep running.'

Bird's Eye peered up into her earnest face and smiled thinly. That's when he felt the watcher's presence, stronger than ever.

He's the one. All this is his work.

They gained the corner. But, to their horror, the nightmare was not over. Immediately in front of them, a Wolver was crouching, ready to pounce. Bird's Eye had been so preoccupied, he hadn't registered its presence.

'Mother,' he murmured as the Wolver advanced. 'Just in case we don't make it, I love you.'

BOOK ONE

The Book of the Game

In a few months every teenager on the planet will be playing . . . Each individual will face his or her own Armageddon. One minute some wretched teenager will be slaying demons, the next the real thing will be in his bedroom. Shadow of the Minotaur

The Book of the Game

1

A universe away there was another teenage boy. Though Bird's Eye didn't know it yet, their destinies were bound together like the strands of a cable, fragile on their own but immensely strong when combined. It would be some time before their paths crossed, but when they did it would be in a fight to the death.

Maybe even beyond.

But that was in the future, and just then Phoenix Graves was more concerned with the present. He was a tall, athletic-looking boy, dark-haired and sallow-skinned. He looked much older than his fourteen years. There was something about his face, a premature seriousness and intensity. He had grown up before his time. In the late afternoon light that lanced across the kitchen, he was reading a computer game magazine as if his life depended on it. A single sentence leapt out at him.

'Death of a computer game designer.'

At first there had been nothing in the latest issue of *Gamestation* to alarm him. Quite the opposite. Phoenix had flicked through the usual features: Hot Stuff, Game Gear, Specials and Cheats before starting on the Reviews. He had turned the pages with some apprehension, before opening the centre spread on the kitchen table. One review in particular made pleasant reading:

The Minotaur bellows in the depths of the labyrinth. The Medusa hisses in the depths of a distant cavern. You are embarking on *The Legendeer: Shadow of the Minotaur,* our five-star hit of the autumn. This is super-charged mythology for *aficionados* and novices alike. You don't need a fistful of GCSEs to enjoy this game, just nerves of steel! The 3D graphics are sleek and convincing and you will be gripped by the astonishing realism of the game environment.

Phoenix smiled. He had played the game. How he had played it! In fact, he had been the first person to log on to *The Legendeer.* His dad had had a hand in designing it, and had used Phoenix as a human guinea pig. But it was the next line which turned his slight, wary smile into a triumphant laugh:

The only disappointment will be that the widely rumoured revolutionary game kit, the Parallel Reality suit giving a feel-around, fear-around sensation has failed to materialize, causing some embarrassment to its manufacturer Magna-com. The suit was meant to give the gamer the illusion of being right there *inside* the game. But don't be put off. PR suit or not, *The Legendeer* is as hot a spine-chiller as you will play this millennium!

Phoenix smiled. He knew why the Parallel Reality suit had failed to materialize.
Because I played and I won.
I went into the game and ripped out its heart.
The game is dead, long live the game.
He had waited for this news for weeks, tossing and turning in bed, remembering how he had played. And how the game had played him! He crossed the floor to get a Coke from the fridge, before continuing to browse through the magazine. A sense of self-satisfaction had started to flow through him. He turned to a new page. That's when he saw it, a single column of seriousness amongst the racy gabblespeak of the rest of the magazine.

CHRIS DARKE (1961–2000)

The editorial team of *Gamestation* are saddened to hear of Chris's early death. Chris Darke designed some of the finest games ever released, from *Time Commando* to the legendary *Death Racer V*.

At the time of his death, Chris had just been head-hunted to take the already successful *Legendeer* series to new heights.

Seamless and innovative, Chris's all-action style has thrilled millions of gamers. Our sadness at the news of his death is all the greater given the circumstances. Tragically, Chris met a violent end in his home, by person or persons unknown.

Phoenix frowned as he reread, trying to unpick more information from this briefest of articles. 'It can't be. I won. It can't start all over again.' He almost ran down the hallway and into Dad's study. It took him a couple of minutes to find the cardboard box containing the Parallel Reality suits. Then there they were, the accessory that would transform computer games, actually taking you into the worlds the designers had created. The suit he held up was tissue-thin. It looked like an all-in-one diving outfit, but more flimsy. Phoenix pulled it open, listening to the familiar hiss of its velcro-like fastening. A sound like the serpent in the garden.

'Not again. It can't begin again.' He glanced at the points bracelet that flashed your score. The crystal display was blank. Finally he examined the balaclava-style face mask attached to the top of the suit. It still gave him the creeps. A clinging, inhuman face. It was as expressionless as death. The thought of ever putting the thing on again filled him with disgust.

But he didn't have to. It was over. Wasn't it?'

While he was repacking the suit, he heard the door. 'Mum? Dad?' There was no answer. Somebody was there, but they weren't answering. There was something about the silence that put him on edge.

He hurried back down the hallway. 'Mum?' He found her in the kitchen, going through her handbag. 'Mum, what's wrong?'

She threw the bag down in exasperation. 'I had a train timetable for London. Where can I have put it?'

'London,' said Phoenix. 'Why London?'

'It's your grandfather. He is very ill.' Phoenix stared at her, demanding more information. 'It's cancer, Phoenix. Grandpa's got cancer.'

'Has he got to have an operation or something?'

A catch came into Mum's voice. 'There's nothing they can do, except ease the pain. It's terminal. He's going to die.'

Phoenix continued to stare. He was thinking of the kindly old man who had come to London in the sixties to make a living, and built a Greek restaurant business out of nothing. 'I'm sorry, Mum.'

She put her hands on his shoulders, and looked into his dark brown eyes. 'Listen, I only heard an hour ago. Your grandmother got me on my mobile at work. It was a terrible shock. I'm going down to stay with them for a few days. They need all the support they can get right now. You'll be fine with your dad.'

Phoenix smiled. 'Of course I will.' The obituary piece in the magazine was still hovering somewhere at the back of his mind, but it no longer seemed so important. He certainly couldn't burden Mum with it now.

'I'm going to pack,' said Mum, snapping a purple band round her mane of raven-black hair. 'Would you do a quick tidy-up?' In a crisis, Mum always resorted to tidying up. It was one of her coping strategies. She indicated the magazines strewn on the table. 'You can put those in your room for a start.'

As Phoenix gathered up the mags, he was desperate to tell her that it might not be over. That the deadly game had come back to life.

Phoenix had cleared the surfaces and was washing the dishes when Dad burst through the door.

'Is Mum back?'

'Yes, she's upstairs packing.'

'She's told you then?' Phoenix nodded. 'This is all we need. After . . .' His voice trailed off. 'Still, at least that's over.'

Phoenix followed Dad with his eyes. *But what if it isn't? What if it's about to begin all over again?*

Six weeks ago – is that all it was? – he had worn that Parallel Reality suit the magazine had talked about, felt it clinging as though it was a second skin, creeping around him like the tendrils of some monstrous plant. He had played the game. Maybe the magazine was right. Maybe *The Legendeer* had been rendered safe, a mere entertainment.

But those few short weeks ago, it had been all too real. It had transported him physically into a world of demons, monsters and savage gods. He had learned that losing the game meant losing your life.

'Phoenix?' Dad was calling from the top of the stairs. 'I'm going to run your mum down to the station. Would you stay and wait by the phone? I'm expecting a call from that job interview.'

Phoenix watched his parents hurrying off. He waved sadly. Mention of the job interview brought it all back. When Dad had worked for the mysterious games company Magna-com, he had helped develop *The Legendeer*.

When he had played the game and found out that it was really playing him.

Just like Chris Darke.

Dusk was gathering by the time Dad pulled into the driveway.

'Dad,' said Phoenix meeting him at the front door, 'there's something I have to show you.'

'Not now, eh?' said John Graves. 'I'm tired and I'm hungry.

Did you take a call about the job?' Dad wasn't thinking demons. He was thinking mortgage. Phoenix winced. The job. He should have mentioned that first. Butter the old man up with the good news.

'Yes, you got it. They're sending you a contract in the next post.' Dad smiled weakly. Mum's news had obviously taken the shine off his success on the job front. 'I could whip up an omelette for you,' said Phoenix, keen to make amends. 'Ham and mushroom be OK?'

'Son, you're a life-saver. That would be great. I'll take a quick shower while you're rustling it up.'

Phoenix listened to the spit of fat in the pan and the sound of water running in the bathroom. He hated having to wait, but he knew it would be wise to hold back on the obituary, at least until Dad had eaten.

'Your mother's devastated,' said Dad, padding across the kitchen in his dressing gown still towelling his shock of ginger hair. 'She hero-worships her dad. They're such a close family.' He hung the towel over the radiator. 'Looks like we'll just have to muddle along without her for a while.'

'Coffee?' asked Phoenix.

'Love one.'

Phoenix approached the table, stirring a mug of instant. 'Dad, I need to show you something.'

John Graves immediately recognized the tone of voice. 'Not in trouble at school, are you?'

'No,' said Phoenix, 'School's fine. I'll get it.' He returned with the magazine and laid it on the table in front of Dad, open at the review page.

'What am I supposed to be looking at?'

Phoenix pointed to the obituary for Chris Darke. 'That.'

Dad shook his head. 'And . . . ?'

'Read it, Dad,' Phoenix, pleaded. 'Read it properly. There. *The Legendeer*. It's the same thing that happened to us.'

'It can't be,' said Dad. 'We stopped him . . . it . . . whatever it was that dragged us into that awful game.' But try as he

18

might, he couldn't deny what was there in front of him in bold print. 'I don't believe it,' he said. 'Not again.'

But it was true. It had begun.

Again.

2

The supermarket was packed the following evening. It was the only one in Brownleigh and the entire population of the small market town seemed to be there.

'No wonder your mum comes back in such a state,' said Dad. 'It's like the chariot race from *Ben Hur*. I swear some of these trollies have scythes attached. Still, let's see if us boys can make a decent job of doing the shopping.' Phoenix saw through the forced gaiety. Dad was trying to keep both their minds off the game.

'I'll tell you what you've forgotten,' said Phoenix, consulting the shopping list they had drawn up. 'Milk. It's two aisles back.' He was one of those three bowls of cereal a day teenagers so milk was a big deal. Dad started to manoeuvre the trolley. 'No,' said Phoenix, 'I'll go. How many should I get?'

'Make it two,' said Dad. 'Only the four-pinters, mind. Those big six-pinters don't fit in our fridge.'

Phoenix nodded and backtracked. As he turned the aisle, his heart missed a beat. There, right in front of him was Steve Adams' mother. Seeing her unexpectedly like that brought to mind the key players in the deadly game he had entered. Phoenix, Dad, Laura . . . and Adams. Phoenix turned furtively and was about to make his way back to Dad when she spotted him.

'Just a moment. It is you isn't it? You're the Graves boy. Please wait.' Phoenix just wanted to escape. 'I know you and Steven didn't get on, but if you know anything, anything at all, you have to tell me.' Phoenix was aware of other shoppers turning and staring. 'Please, just the slightest detail you forgot to tell the police. It's been weeks. I can't bear not knowing what's happened to him.'

Phoenix wanted to tell her what he knew. But how? How do you explain to a mother that her son has been transported into a world which dances to Evil's fiddle – and that he loves every minute of it! Phoenix remembered the last time he had seen her son. The moment when Adams chose to stay in the game, rather than come home.

'I'm sorry, Mrs Adams, but I haven't seen him.' His reply, so obviously a lie, provoked a change in Mrs Adams. Her eyes narrowed. Phoenix saw her suspicion. 'You do know something, don't you?'

In his mind's eye, Phoenix saw Adams retreating into the darkness, returning to *him*. 'No, Mrs Adams. Honestly, I don't know what's happened to him.'

'Please,' she said. 'I can see it in your face.' She opened her purse. 'Money! I can pay you. How much do you want?'

'Mrs Adams. Please don't.' She was advancing on him, purse open. Then there was another voice.

'Margaret!'

Mrs Adams turned, and seeing her husband, she immediately burst into tears and buried her face into his shoulder. 'He knows something, Brian,' she sobbed. 'I'm sure he does. But he won't tell. How could he be so cruel?' Mr Adams patted his wife on the back and gestured to Phoenix to go. On shaky legs, Phoenix found his way back to Dad.

'So where's the milk?' Phoenix stared dumbly at his empty hands. 'Well?'

'I ran into Mrs Adams. She started giving me the third degree.'

'You didn't tell her anything, did you?'

'Of course not, what could I say?'

Dad sighed. 'The shopping can wait another day. I'll come back by myself tomorrow evening. When the coast is clear.'

Phoenix nodded gratefully and they made for the exit.

He couldn't put thoughts of the obituary and the game out of his mind. The following evening, after Dad had gone out to make the return journey to the supermarket, Phoenix slipped into the study and searched for Dad's copy of *The Legendeer*. It wasn't hidden, or locked away. The game really was harmless.

It wasn't without misgivings that Phoenix downloaded it, but there was nothing to arouse his suspicions. The labyrinth where he had fought a life-and-death battle with the Minotaur, the cavern where he had beheaded the Gorgon, Medusa, they were graphic images on the screen. Vivid and scary, but not real.

Now for the real test, he thought. Slowly, with the sort of care you devote to something very precious, or very dangerous, he donned the PR suit, plugging it into the computer. The suit was the passport to terror. Phoenix remembered the way he had been transported into the game, the brilliant portal of light, the flashing numbers. This time, nothing happened.

Nothing at all.

The gate is closed. There is nowhere to go.

With relief pulsating through him, he slipped off the suit, folded it, and put it back in its box. 'Round one to us,' said Phoenix out loud. 'But what about round two?'

Had he returned to the study just five minutes later he would have got his answer. The computer was on. It had switched on by itself. What's more, the screen was covered with a familiar blizzard of marching numbers. It was the encrypted code from another world, a spiralling sequence of threes, sixes and nines. It was the demon inside the machine, and this is what it had to say:

So you want to play?'
Then I, the Gamesmaster, will be happy to oblige.
It has been a while, Legendeer, at least as far as you are concerned. To a youth of fourteen summers, the weeks pass

slowly. But to one such as I who was there before the pyramids and will remain long after the sun burns out, weeks or months amount to no more than a speck of dust in the eye of time.

Do you miss the clash of battle, the thrill of terror? Or is it fear that draws you back? Fear of me. Fear of what I can do.

You feel my presence still, don't you? Every time a flame gutters, every time the wind moans, every time you switch off the light, you sense me behind you. Every time the computer hums, you feel my presence.

The Gamesmaster.

You are right to be afraid. You quite ruined the first round of the game, but if you imagine you have conquered me then think again.

In my long march to rebirth and freedom, I have suffered many setbacks.

Even so, my latest plans are well-advanced.

Here I come, ready or not.

3

Phoenix felt something as he passed the doorway to the study the following evening. How to describe it – a chill, a tingling, a touch maybe? It was one of those moments when the walls of safe, everyday reality come down to reveal the shadows beyond. But he had no time to dwell on the unsettling sensation. The chirrup of the telephone was insistent. 'OK, OK, I'm coming.' He covered the mouthpiece and called down the hallway into the living room. 'Laura, would you get me something to drink?'

He heard her shifting out of her chair. He marvelled for a moment at the contrast in the house. First, there was the ordinariness and predictability of its routine. He could locate where anybody was simply by the way the floorboards creaked. Then there was the disturbance that gnawed at its heart, the possibility of a gate to terror suddenly opening.

'Hello? Mum! Good to hear your voice. How's Grandpa?'

'Not so good. He doesn't grumble much, but he isn't a bit well. He gets tired easily. He's lost weight, too. It's terrible seeing him like this. He was always such a strong man. Invincible, or so I always thought.'

'When are you coming home?'

'That's what I was calling about. Is Dad in?'

'No,' Phoenix replied. 'He's got a meeting at work.'

He heard Mum's breath catch. 'Of course, the new job. It slipped my mind completely. I haven't even congratulated him. There hasn't been room in my mind for anything except your grandfather. You must think I'm very selfish.'

'No, I don't,' Phoenix replied. 'Any message for Dad?'

'I'd like the two of you to come down this weekend. Grandma would appreciate it.'

'Sure,' said Phoenix, 'I'll tell him.'

'You wouldn't mind coming down?'

'No Mum, not a bit.'

'Papa's been asking after you. He mentions you in the same breath as Andreas.'

There was a moment's silence.

'Grandpa actually said his name?'

'Yes. That's twice in a few weeks. It must be the illness. They say looking death in the face makes you relive your past.'

Andreas. It was a name that meant so much in the family. Finally Mum spoke again. 'Any news at your end?'

Phoenix let the events of the last two days run through his mind: the obituary, the encounter with Mrs Adams. Neither of them were what Mum wanted to hear just then. 'No, we're managing fine. Dad's even done the ironing. Shirts and everything.'

'That I'd like to see.'

Mum sounded weary. The hollowness in her voice made Phoenix's heart ache. 'I'll go now, son. Ask Dad to phone me back about the weekend. Promise you won't forget?'

'Promise.'

Phoenix returned to the living room, hurrying just a little as he passed the study door. He could feel the darkness reaching out to him.

'Your mum?' asked Laura, holding out a can of Seven Up.

'Yes. She sounds really down.'

'I'm not surprised. Did you mention what's happened?'

Phoenix looked at Laura, taking in the dreadlocked hair, the deep black-brown of her skin, the slightly blueish tone that showed under the electric light. She was tall and striking, one of the headturners at Brownleigh High. 'How could I? She's got enough on her plate.'

Laura tossed a copy of *The Guardian* on to the coffee table.

'That's it. Two weeks' worth of newspapers and not a single mention of Chris Darke.'

'And your Dad doesn't keep them any further back?'

Laura shook her head. 'He's a stickler for routine. A leftover from his time in the Nigerian civil service. Keeps them exactly two weeks, then gives them to the paper collection. I suppose we should try the library next. It'll have to be the weekend, though. Our parents won't want us going into town straight from school.'

Phoenix nodded. 'We can't do much about it until Saturday.' He glanced down at the newspapers. 'Still, it was worth a try. I just thought we might strike lucky.' Then he cursed, low, under his breath.

'Now what?'

'I just thought, I won't be able to go to the library this weekend. I'll be in London. You know, my grandpa. There's no way I can get out of it.'

Laura smiled. 'I'll do the research. I'm very capable.'

It was Phoenix's turn to smile. Just how capable he had discovered when they played the game. She had endured all the terrors of the myth-world and come out smiling – just! That wasn't capable, that was heroic.

'I know you are. I'd like to have gone along with you.'

'I'll manage,' said Laura, before changing the subject. 'Phoenix, how far do you think Chris Darke got with the game?'

'No idea. There isn't much to go on. Yet . . .'

'Yes?'

Phoenix searched for the words. 'Sometimes feelings are stronger than facts. It's this instinct I have inside me. It tells me to be on my guard. Something's coming.'

'You're scaring me.'

Phoenix toyed with his drink. 'I'm scaring myself. You won't believe what I've done, but I've had my PR suit on again.'

'Whatever for?'

'I suppose I wanted to convince myself the game really is harmless. That it wasn't going to start all over again.'

Laura leaned forward. 'Did you? Convince yourself, I mean.'

Phoenix shook his head. 'All I did by touching those things was to bring it all back. The labyrinth, the poison cave, the fear. The Gamesmaster's still out there, Laura. I can feel him. It's anything but over.'

Laura shuddered involuntarily. 'Hey, look at the time. I'd better go.'

Phoenix stood at the door, watching her disappear into the evening mist. He was at a loss after that, flitting from one thing to another, unable to settle. Dad wouldn't be home for hours and the emptiness of the house made him anxious. He thought about doing his homework, but he just couldn't concentrate. He switched on the TV and spent ten minutes channel-surfing, before giving it up as a bad job. Three times he visited the kitchen, picking at peanuts and taking a couple of bites out of an apple before dropping it into the bin. In the end there was only one thing which would put his mind to rest. He climbed the stairs to his parents' room and crossed the floor to Mum's bedside table. He slid open the drawer and took out the journal.

Andreas' journal.

He carried it downstairs and started to read.

Andreas was Grandpa's twin brother. Their story was unremarkable enough at first, just two boys growing up in rural Greece. Then came adolescence. Grandpa did all the normal things: he got into mischief, had fights, became interested in girls. Andreas was different. As the years went on, he became withdrawn and suffered long bouts of ill-health. Some days he was paralysed by merciless, blinding headaches and would spend the daylight hours lying in a darkened room. Then, when he was fourteen, the haunting started, the visions that drove him to the brink of madness. Despite constant nightmares and long spells of illness, he managed to become a schoolteacher. Everyone hoped that,

27

once Andreas had grown to manhood, he would leave his strange moods behind. He didn't. They just became longer and more intense. Phoenix opened the journal.

I want to sleep, read one entry, *to close my eyes and never open them again. I see them all the time now, the magic numbers, the demons. It is more than I can bear.*

'The numbers,' Phoenix said out loud, 'That's the link.'

Gradually, the days when Andreas seemed possessed multiplied, while the good days, the days when he could function as an ordinary man became fewer and fewer, eventually dwindling almost to nothing. Finally, it all became too much. Andreas suffered a breakdown and was committed to an asylum.

'But you weren't mad, were you?' Phoenix murmured. 'Or else I am, as well. The headaches you suffered, I have them too. The nightmares that haunted you, I've experienced them. The things you saw. I've seen them too. I saw them in the game.'

Phoenix read the tell-tale entry, the page he had read and reread so many times since first playing *The Legendeer*.

The more I think about it, the sickliness, the band of pain, the strange waking fever that has been with me all my life, the more I realize that it has something to do with the ghosts. When they gather, when they step out of the shimmering light and speak to me, then I understand. I belong to their world. I always have.

For all time, I will be a stranger inside my own skin. I have a mission. For every ghost that believes in life and justice and warns me of the dangers of the gate, there are others who are filled with death and destruction. They are knocking at the door. But they will not pass me. I am the Legendeer.

My task is to keep the gate closed, to keep out the demon legions. Though it breaks my heart every day of my life, I will never give up my vigil. To leave my post would be to abandon this world to horror.

28

'But a computer game that relives my family's past,' said Phoenix. 'How can that be?'

There were no answers in that silent house, only questions.

What was the link between a tormented schoolteacher in Greece in the 1960s and a macabre computer game almost forty years later?

What would Andreas have said if he had seen *The Legendeer*? Most importantly, how could his family have deserted him and locked him up like that? A man who was lucid and sane, imprisoned in a madhouse cell.

Phoenix sat back and closed his eyes. The family's trip to their home village came flooding back. He saw the cypress groves and the low stone walls surrounding Andreas' house. Then the house itself. The pictures of demons, numbers all over the walls.

No wonder they thought you were mad.

'But you were the only one who was sane,' said Phoenix. He closed the journal, but he couldn't close the cover on the family secret. It would always be there, the knowledge that in the terrifying spaces between everyday reality, there were other, parallel worlds. And in those worlds all the nightmare creatures that have stalked the minds of men go in search of prey.

And we are their prey.

Dad got home just before eleven. He was having to work late and even then his day wasn't done. The office was an hour's drive from Brownleigh, ninety minutes in the rush hour. He found Phoenix sleeping fitfully on the couch. Moving quietly across the floor so as not to disturb his sleeping son, John Graves switched off the TV and sat opposite. He had been there a couple of minutes before he noticed the grimy volume beside Phoenix on the arm of the couch.

'What's this you've been reading?' he murmured. Casting his eyes over the page, he paused, apprehension stealing through him. Unlike his wife and son, he couldn't read

Greek, but he could read the scrap of paper Phoenix was using as a bookmark. On it, Phoenix had translated an entry which read:

At least I know that, no matter how they haunt me, there is no way the demons can infect this beautiful world of ours.

John Graves slowly shook his head. 'If only we were so sure,' he said, 'if only it were true.'

4

It was just after seven o'clock the following evening when the front doorbell rang.

'Who's that?' said Phoenix, consulting the wall clock. 'Not double-glazing salesmen again.' He was in luck. The smiling face that greeted him on the doorstep belonged to Laura.

'Guess what I've got?' she said, waving a scrap of paper under his nose. 'Only Chris Darke's phone number.'

'You're kidding! I thought we'd agreed we wouldn't be able to get to the library on a weekday.'

'I didn't go to the library. But I happened to mention the story to Dad.' She held up her hand. 'Don't worry, I didn't give anything away. Dad remembered it. He's got one of those minds. Always does really well on quiz programmes. Anyway, it was there locked away at the back of his mind. He remembered the Darke murder and where it happened, so I called directory enquiries. Three Darkes listed, only one a C. Darke.'

Phoenix led her inside.

'OK,' she said, 'So do we call?'

Phoenix glanced at the number on the crumpled piece of paper. 'S'pose so.'

'You don't sound very enthusiastic.'

'What do we say?' asked Phoenix. 'Mrs Darke, could you confirm that your husband was killed by demons; you know, the ones that live in the computer game he was designing?'

'It's your call,' said Laura. 'You're the one who's convinced something's happening.' Phoenix took the number and laid it

31

on the hall table. Instinctively, he glanced at Dad's computer, the doorway into the Gamesmaster's myth-world. Laura followed his gaze. 'Spooky, isn't it?' she said. 'Considering what happened last time.'

Phoenix bit his bottom lip and lifted the handset. The thought of hordes of demons massing on the other side of the screen prompted him to action. 'I still don't know what to say.'

'Can't help you,' said Laura. 'I wouldn't like to do it.'

Phoenix punched out the number. When the phone was picked up at the other end, his throat went completely dry. 'Mrs Darke?' he asked croakily.

'I'll get her.' It was a boy, nine or ten maybe. 'Mum,' he called. 'It's for you.' Phoenix and Laura exchanged glances, then Mrs Darke was on the line.

'Hello?'

'Mrs Darke, you don't know me, but I read about what happened to your husband . . . in *Gamestation* magazine.' He hesitated, wondering how to continue. 'I wonder, could you tell me about the game he was working on?'

The voice at the other end was suspicious. 'Who is this? Did you know my husband?'

'No, I didn't. But I think we've got something in common. I know about *The Legendeer*. Do you know if he finished it?'

Suspicion had turned to fear. Mrs Darke's voice was full of emotion. 'If this is some sort of sick joke, I don't think it's funny. Who are you?' Phoenix looked at Laura. This was going seriously wrong. 'If you call again, I'll be contacting the police. Do you understand?'

'Yes,' said Phoenix, 'I understand.' He replaced the phone.

'That was a bit of a disaster, wasn't it?' said Laura, stating the obvious.

'On a scale of one to ten,' said Phoenix, 'it was zero. She thought I was a crank caller.' They were still standing by the telephone when they heard a car pulling into the driveway. 'That'll be Dad,' said Phoenix, 'Don't mention any of this. He'd go ballistic.'

'Hello? Phoenix?'

'Hi, Dad. We're here.'

'Oh, hello Laura. I didn't know you were coming round again.'

'Spur of the moment,' said Laura. The small talk was interrupted a moment later by the shrill ring of the phone. Dad picked up.

'I beg your pardon? A call from this number? Are you sure?' He glanced at Phoenix.

'Oh great,' groaned Phoenix. 'She must have rung 1471. Call-back.'

'He asked what?' exclaimed Dad. 'I really must apologize, Mrs Darke. Yes, most upsetting. Don't worry, I assure you it won't happen again. Yes, yes, I'll speak to him. Do accept my sincerest apologies.'

Dad replaced the phone and glared at Phoenix. 'Have you taken leave of your senses? You rang Chris Darke's widow!'

'I had to know, Dad. I had to be sure . . .'

Dad opened his briefcase and flourished a manila folder. 'If you'd bothered to ask, I've looked into it already. There was no reason to go upsetting the poor woman.'

Phoenix stared back in disbelief. 'You checked up! But I thought . . .'

'That I wasn't interested?'

'Something like that.'

'Just because I haven't talked about it much, doesn't mean I'm not concerned.'

It was Phoenix's turn to be angry. 'You could have told me!'

'Yes,' said Dad, a hint of guilt in his voice, 'I suppose I could. I've had so much on my mind. The new job, your grandfather . . .'

'So what have you found out?'

'Come into the living room and I'll show you.'

They were able to piece together Chris Darke's story from the newspaper clippings and snippets from the various game

33

magazines. Darke had been headhunted by Magna-com to produce their latest game, a sequel to *The Legendeer*.

'It was so strange finding out about Darke,' said Dad grimly, remembering the torment the game had dragged him into. 'It was like reliving what happened to me. Though Darke didn't know it, he was stepping into my shoes. Only he didn't know how dangerous it was.'

'Vampires,' said Laura, reading the excerpts.

'I beg your pardon?'

'The game. It isn't the Greek myths this time. It's vampires.'

'Oh, I see. Yes, seems the Gamesmaster is moving on to a different set of legends. Maybe by defeating him we made that last world useless for his plans.'

'But just look at the new one,' said Phoenix. 'A parallel world peopled by the undead. And trying to break into the land of the living.'

Laura shuddered. 'If anything, it sounds worse than last time.'

'Look here,' said Dad. 'Darke already had a working title for it – *Legendeer 2: Vampyr Legion*.'

Phoenix scanned the cuttings gloomily. 'I knew it wasn't over.'

'We're luckier than Darke,' said Dad. 'We got out alive. Poor man. What a terrible way to die.'

Laura and Phoenix exchanged glances. 'Is there something you haven't told us?'

Dad tugged nervously at his russet beard. 'The police found him lying on the floor of his studio. There's a mention in one of the reports of him being at his work-desk at the time of the attack. Reading between the lines, I'd say he was wearing his Parallel Reality suit, and it was still plugged in to the PC.'

'You mean he died while he was in the game?' asked Laura.

'No, not in the game. There were signs of a struggle in the studio. A broken lamp, some overturned furniture. He fought for his life, but not while he was in the world of the game. His killer had followed him back.'

'A demon? But how?'

'Not a demon,' said Dad. 'If they could break through, the Gamesmaster would already have won. No, not a demon but somebody who serves them.' He handed Phoenix a cutting from a local newspaper. There were two leads not mentioned anywhere else. One was an intriguing rumour of cult involvement, that had been kept out of the rest of the coverage. The other mentioned the sighting of a youth in his teens leaving the house.

'I know it seems stupid,' said Phoenix. 'But for a moment I actually thought it might be Adams.'

'Now that is paranoia,' said Laura. 'Even Steve couldn't do something like this.'

'Are you sure about that?'

It was a while before any of them spoke and when Phoenix finally broke the silence it was to utter a single word:

'Vampires.'

5

That Thursday night was the last Phoenix and John Graves would spend in the house before travelling to London. As the small hours of Friday morning dawned, an eery electronic glow filled the study. It touched the cardboard box containing the PR suits, the storage units, the bookshelves, the curtains. The computer switched itself on again, conducting its sinister monologue in the dull, dead silence. The only sound was the wheezing of the north wind outside.

Bravo Legendeer!

So you know about Darke. He got too inquisitive, and curiosity killed the cat. That's right, Darke wasn't satisfied developing the game. He had to stick his nose in where it wasn't wanted. Just like you once did.

But Darke didn't have your luck. He saw, he ran, he died. He completed the game on the night of his death. It has gone for pressing. I am just weeks away from victory, and there isn't a thing you can do to stop me.

Enjoy the bliss of ignorance. Sleep while you still can.

6

The drive home from London was a quiet affair. Even at the best of times, visiting a sick relative wasn't going to be easy. But these weren't the best of times. Grandma had cried most of the time, retreating upstairs to keep her lonely vigil over Grandpa. Great aunt Sophia had glared at everyone, as if daring them to mention her *other* brother. It was as if they had spent the entire weekend at Grandma's avoiding one name, Andreas. Mum had cooked, fussed and made endless cups of coffee, anything to keep busy. Dad found himself a chair in the corner of the living room and buried himself in a book. As for Phoenix, he'd scanned the family photographs, imagining Grandpa's twin brother, Andreas, the family member nobody ever mentioned. But he didn't say his name either. Instead he brooded, wondering how the family could have allowed him to be locked up like a madman, somebody they were supposed to have loved. Now, as the miles rolled by, neither Mum, Dad nor Phoenix felt much like talking. Each of them was, in their own way, preoccupied with matters of life and death. Instead of talking, they kept their minds busy, Dad with his driving, Mum with a poetry anthology and Phoenix with his vampires. He had just reached a chapter which seemed to have more to do with military hardware than with myth.

The crossbow, or arbalest, (he read) one of the key killing tools of the vampire slayer. It is a means of delivering a stake through the demon's heart from a distance and with the force of 20 men. Used in war and sport in medieval

Europe, it consists of a wooden stock, with a bow made of wood, iron or steel crossing it at right angles. The bolts it fires are known as quarrels.

A little further on, an excerpt from a particularly lurid short story made him sit up. It was a reworking of the old vampire theme, but with a fascinating difference.

'Know this, Fernando,' said the old priest. 'The vampyr has neither fear of the holy cloth, nor of the crucifix. The cross it fears is yonder bow, set in the shape of the crucifix. Waste not your time throwing holy water. To destroy the creature you must drive a point directly through its heart, rend its corrupted body asunder or expose it to the blazing intensity of sunlight. Those are the three paths to victory over the Beast.'

Phoenix immediately relayed the information to his parents, expecting them to greet it with the same fascination he had.
'What *are* you reading?' Mum asked. 'Dear me, hasn't this family had enough of demons?' The moment the words left her lips the atmosphere in the car changed. Dad became more intent on his driving. Phoenix buried his face in his book, angry with himself for letting his tongue run away with him. 'What's happened?' Mum demanded, her voice filling with dread. 'What are you keeping from me?'
'Nothing,' said Dad. 'Honestly, it's nothing.'
'Don't treat me like a child,' said Mum. 'I knew there was something when I phoned home. You were so tight-lipped, Phoenix. Not like you at all.'
'Just drop it, eh, Mum,' said Phoenix.
'No,' she retorted. 'I will not drop it. I am as much part of this family as either of you. I have lived this nightmare as much as either of you.'
Phoenix caught Dad's eye in the rear-view mirror. They exchanged a brief nod. It was time to come clean. After all, it

38

was Mum who had revealed the truth about Andreas, Mum who had witnessed Phoenix's previous adventures on the computer screen. They had all shared the first chapter of the terror. They would face this new episode together.

'We'd better talk,' said Dad. 'I'll pull in at the next services.'

In the end, Phoenix thought it better to let Dad do the explaining. Leaving his parents speaking in hushed voices over two hot chocolates, he wandered round the building. After drifting aimlessly for a few minutes, looking down at the speeding lanes of traffic then strolling round the telephone boxes and cash machines, he found himself at the entrance to the shop. He browsed along the bookshelves then moved on to the magazine racks. He honed in on the new edition of *Gamestation* straight away. Of course, the last Friday in the month. He had his copy on order. It would have been lying on the hall mat all weekend, waiting for him. But there was no way he would be able to hang on until he got home.

Imagine if there were something in there, a mention of Darke or the game. He had to know right away. As he laid the magazine on the counter, he couldn't help but think it was some sort of sick joke. Demons, man's most ancient fear, were at the door. And what was going to let them through? Only our most modern and sophisticated technological advance – the computer.

'That'll be three pounds fifty,' said the woman behind the till. 'Computer games, eh? My son's really into all that.'

That's the trouble, thought Phoenix. Everybody is. He re-ran the nightmare vision. In a matter of months, maybe even weeks hundreds of thousands of kids, maybe even millions, would be sitting in front of a computer game, battling its demons. Then the demon would take form. That was the endgame: millions of demons pouring through millions of computer screens.

A world invaded.

A nightmare triumphant.

39

No sooner was he out of the shop than he tore off the cellophane wrapper and discarded it. News. Nothing there. His heart started to beat a little more slowly.

Reviews. Still nothing. It took two readings to satisfy himself that he was right, but there was no doubt about it. *Vampyr Legion* wasn't on sale yet.

We've got time.

He had reached page 62 before he came across the section which would turn his blood to ice. It was a glossy pullout called 'In the Pipeline'. And there it was, the news he had been dreading.

Magna-com's latest is ahead of schedule. *Vampyr Legion*, the much-anticipated second part of the *Legendeer* series should be in the outlets soon, just in time for Christmas.

If anything, the tragic and mysterious death of its original designer, Chris Darke, has only added to the interest around its launch, giving the state of the art game a money-spinning air of notoriety. After *Shadow of the Minotaur*, we know what to expect from Magna-com, great 3D graphics and story lines to make you quake.

The only question now is: will they finally be able to introduce the revolutionary Parallel Reality suit? Our sources tell us that *Vampyr Legion* really will slay us!

For a moment Phoenix could barely breathe. It was coming.

He was coming. The Gamesmaster's boast, that soon demons would pour from the screen of every computer, was about to come true.

'Christmas,' he said, not noticing an elderly couple watching him with some amusement. As he dashed off to tell his parents the news, the couple exchanged smiles.

'Kids,' said the old lady. 'They live in a dreamworld all their own.'

'I know,' her husband replied. 'You'd swear it was real.'

7

'I beg your pardon?' said Dad, as if unable to believe his own ears. He put down the bundle of mail he had just picked up off the hall mat. 'You did what?' The conversation they had begun on the motorway was still in full flow as they walked into the house.

'I wore one of the suits,' Phoenix replied, 'I was worried by the Darke obituary.' He saw Dad's expression change. He decided to avoid a row. 'At least that's the way it seemed. So I decided to check the game out for myself.' He said it as if hooking himself up to *The Legendeer* was the most natural thing in the world.

'Have you forgotten what happened the last time you wore one of those things?' Mum said. 'I had to watch helplessly while you . . . You could have been killed. Oh, Phoenix, how could you? And without telling us!'

Despite the third degree, Phoenix couldn't help noticing Dad staring intently at one of the letters in the pile he had dropped onto the hall table.

'But I knew it was safe,' Phoenix retorted. 'At least, I was 99 per cent sure. You said it yourself Dad; by beating the Gamesmaster last time round we destroyed the threat.' Dad had taken the letter and slipped it into his pocket. He looked startled when Phoenix said his name. 'We turned the first part of *The Legendeer* into an ordinary game,' Phoenix said, irritated by the way Dad was continuing to leaf through his letters. 'Even with the PR suit on, nothing happened.'

41

'No,' said Dad, 'But it could have done. You took a stupid risk.'

But you know I wasn't in danger. What's going on here? Why are you so upset? Phoenix saw something new in Dad's face, blind, unreasoning fear. All of a sudden, disappointment had turned to anger.

But why?

'Don't make excuses, Phoenix,' Dad snapped. 'You were forbidden to ever wear those infernal suits again.'

'You can't just blame him, John,' said Mum. 'I thought we'd agreed to destroy them. Then nobody could play.'

Dad looked away.

'John, why didn't you?'

There was a long silence.

'I know why,' said Phoenix. 'You weren't sure, were you Dad? You thought, maybe it wasn't all over. Maybe it was going to start all over again. That's it, isn't it? You thought we might have to return to the world of the game one day.'

Dad looked suddenly older, his face lined and grey. 'Yes, maybe I did.'

'And you were right. If we don't go into his world, how *do* we fight the Gamesmaster?'

'We find Darke's colleagues,' Dad replied. 'We find the game's manufacturer. We tell them what we know. I know you don't think much of my efforts, Phoenix, but that's what I've been trying to do.'

'But it isn't enough,' cried Phoenix. 'You can find as many designers and programmers as you like. The Gamesmaster will always come up with somebody else to carry on his work. We thought we'd won last time, but we hadn't. We've got to go back into his world and finish the job. The myth-world is real, Dad, as real as this one. You know that feeling when you get up in the night, and you think something's behind you? Well, it isn't our imagination. It's true. There's a nightmare world right behind us, *many* nightmare worlds, and every one as real as this one. That's where the battle is to be won or lost.' But Phoenix himself was fighting a losing battle. Mum delivered the fatal blow.

'No Phoenix, your dad's right. We have to try his way first. If we can't stop the game's production, then we can try your way.'

'Yes,' Phoenix said desperately, 'And by then we will have wasted so much time, nothing will be able to stop him. Could you live with that on your conscience?'

'Listen to me, Phoenix,' said Dad, his face set. 'Whatever happens, you are not to touch the PR suits. Do you understand me?'

'I understand, but what's the big deal? It's not like we've even got a copy of the new game.' There was a moment's silence, as if Phoenix had sworn in church.

'I've said all I've got to say, Phoenix. You let me follow up my leads and you keep out of the study. Do I make myself clear?'

Phoenix tried to argue back, but it was no use. With his parents putting up a united front, he was beaten.

'Sure Dad, it's crystal clear.'

When Phoenix went up to bed at half past ten, Dad was shut up in the study, hammering away at the computer. Phoenix imagined him opening files, sending e-mail, cross-referencing leads. In short, he would be working feverishly, trying to convince himself he was doing *something*. Phoenix sat in his room, resenting his parents for deceiving themselves, he knew trying to beat the Gamesmaster from outside wouldn't work. The Gamesmaster wasn't a virus, a rogue piece of software. He was no artificial intelligence. He was the demon-lord, and the computer was merely a way to open the gate between his world and ours.

'If I can't do it with you,' Phoenix said, 'Then I'll have to do it without you.' He sat a while with his elbows on his knees, face buried in his hands. Then, straightening up, he came to a decision. 'I have to return. I have to track him to his lair, destroy the architect of the game.'

But how? Without a copy of the game, he was shut out, doomed to sit and wait for the storm to break over his head. When Phoenix finally fell asleep, he was worn out, exhausted from wracking his brain for a solution. Whatever he thought, however he turned it this way and that in his mind, without a copy of *Vampyr Legion* there could be no battle. And without battle, there could be no victory.

8

Downstairs in his study, John Graves worked into the night. But not the way Phoenix thought. The moment Dad locked himself in the study, he pulled the letter from his pocket. It was a small, brown bubble envelope. He held it up to the light, inspecting the postmark. After a moment's reflection, he tore it open and read the letter.

Dear Mr Graves,

I'm sorry I was so off-hand with you when you rang me back. I am sure you can understand my distress. After my husband's murder, I didn't know who to turn to, who to trust. Is this what the killer was after?

Dad slid the small disc from the envelope and read the Gothic script: *Vampyr Legion*.

I think the killer got away with the original disc, the one Chris was working on, but he made a back-up copy and sent it to his parents for safe keeping. He had been worried for a long time. He had begun to take all sorts of precautions. I thought it was paranoia. How wrong I was! Chris's dad returned the disc to me at the funeral, so here it is. I have to admit that I don't understand what's going on and why this game led to my husband's death, but you have convinced me that you should have the disc. I am putting my faith in you, Mr Graves. I want you to bring Chris's murderer to justice. Maybe that way I can begin to sleep at night.

> Yours sincerely,
> Ruth Darke

Dad turned the disc between his fingers. He found his attention drawn first to the computer, then to the PR suits in their box. 'What now?' he murmured. 'What now?'

Out in the garden somebody was moving. Over six feet tall, of athletic, muscular build, the stranger was staring intently at the Graves' house. In particular, he was watching the light burning in the study. He took a step forward, compulsively clenching and relaxing his gloved hands. He watched all that night, standing under the flashing stars, the waxing moon, the rushing stormclouds. He saw the study light go off and moved slowly towards the house. Then, just as he reached the window, the light was switched back on. The stranger slipped back into the shadows, darkness against darkness.

Phoenix heard Dad making his way upstairs at about four o'clock. Everything that had happened in the last few months had made Phoenix a light sleeper. Sometimes he would wake up on the hour every hour. Was it the thoughts racing through his mind that jerked him awake, or the nightmares that came to call every time his head touched the pillow?

'Won't sleep now,' he grumbled, and switched on his bedside lamp. He reached for the vampire book, and opened it at the description of the crossbow. As he reread it he felt a draught, a breeze that seemed to sing across the room without even disturbing the curtains. 'Stop it,' he told himself, 'You're just imagining things.'

But as he read the brief chapter, it was as if he was seeing with new eyes. He started to interpret it differently, absorbing the facts as if they were a list of instructions. Each illustration fell into place, disassembling then reassembling the slayer's tool step by lethal step.

'I could make this,' he said excitedly. 'I could actually make this.' Then, a split-second later, the excitement faded from his face. 'But what would be the point? I will never be able to use it. Not without the game.' He put the book face down on the cover and pillowed his head on his palms.

'You're out there,' he said, speaking to the shadows and the cracks on the ceiling, the hints of darkness that crouched all around him. 'I beat you once, but that was only a skirmish, wasn't it? The real battles are still to come.' He could feel the presence. He was downstairs in the circuit boards and the memory of the computer. He was in the sighing wind and the grotesque faces the darkness made on his wallpaper.

You're even in my head.

Then all of a sudden there was something else in his head.

Dad slipped something into his pocket.

Phoenix jerked upright. 'That's right, he did.' Then the realization:

'It was a letter.'

Phoenix closed his eyes and tried to bring it to mind. A package, a small brown package. Then his eyes flashed open.

It couldn't be.

Could it?

Phoenix waited until the clock read 4.33 before he slipped out of bed and made his way downstairs. The worst moment was when he had to turn off the burglar alarm. Even though he closed the door to the cupboard that housed the alarm box, each time he pressed the key it seemed to yelp more loudly. But nobody came downstairs. He was in the clear. Padding down the hall in bare feet, Phoenix paused at the study door.

The lock. What do I do about the lock?

But almost before he had time to think, Phoenix saw the entire lock assembly as if it were part of a child's puzzle. He hurried to the kitchen, came back and rummaged until he found what he was after. Armed with a thin bladed knife, he set about picking the lock. After two or three agonizing minutes, it sprang open. Without ever wondering how he could suddenly spring a lock, he shoved the door open. Once inside, Phoenix searched the computer table, the desk, even the chaotic piles of paperwork.

Nothing. Then his eyes fell on Dad's briefcase. He rattled the catches. It wasn't locked.

The rest was simple: replacing the disc with a blank from Dad's store, copying the words *Vampyr Legion* on to the label in as good an attempt at Gothic script as he could manage, relocking the door and resetting the alarm. Phoenix was back in his room by five o'clock. With the disc safely hidden under a loose floorboard, he slept soundly.

No nightmares this time.

9

Phoenix wasn't going to be hurried. The game could be a trap.

But what if the trap can spring both ways?

He viewed *Vampyr Legion* without wearing the PR suit. He did everything consciously, systematically. Now that he had the disc, he was transformed. He had a say in his own destiny. He wasn't going to dash in headlong, as he had with *Shadow of the Minotaur*. He watched it all, the whole of Level One, from the moment the Vampyrs landed on the mansion house roof, through the frenzied battle in the cellar, to Captain Lawrence's brave sacrifice, and Ann and Bird's Eye's escape.

But that's all he did.

He watched.

He watched mother and son spilling onto the street, half-daring to think they were safe, then confronting the moon-born beast that shook its silver mane and howled eerily. Finally he watched them freeze, Ann and Robert Van Helsing, the Wolver, even time itself, waiting for him, Phoenix, to enter and set it in motion once more.

It hadn't been easy. Every fibre of his being itched to be there, standing between the two fugitives and their unearthly pursuer. But Phoenix had learned how the Gamesmaster thought, how he played with time and space. What the demon-lord was after was *engagement*, a connection with Phoenix's world, his coveted prize. And Ann and Bird's Eye were the bait. So Phoenix bided his time.

I don't need to hurry. I can wait for the connection.

And he had discovered it. It was the moonlight. What else

would it be in a tale of vampires and werewolves? The Van Helsings were hurrying through London's Edwardian streets, their shadows cast crisp and dark by a full, white, swollen moon.

'And our full moon is in two days,' said Phoenix. 'That's when the two worlds come into line. That's when we will write the remaining levels together, you and I, my old enemy.'

Phoenix continued his preparations patiently and in secret. He didn't drop a single hint to Mum or Dad, or even to Laura, his partner in the last adventure.

This time I'm going alone.

Nobody to worry about. Nobody to care about.

It's just you and me, Gamesmaster.

The precious interlude between getting in from school around 3.30 p.m. and Mum arriving from work around 4.30 p.m. became his time. That's when he combed the game for details, that's when he watched every movement of the Vampyr and the Wolver, how they sprang and how they attacked. That's when he moved around the study, shadowing their moves, inventing feints and strategies of his own.

It was also then, in the gathering twilight, that he fashioned the slayer's tool – the arbalest. He did it with a craftsman's eye, carving, mitring, honing. He prepared stock and bowstring, trigger and lever, groove and quarrel. Each part he made with meticulous care, laying it aside just before Mum walked through the door. There was no haste in his work. He was measured, steady. He felt his destiny as if it were as heavy and as solid as the stock of the crossbow. His last task was to give this killing cross a name. Finally, he had it.

He christened it 'Angel of Death.'

10

It was the night of the full moon.

Phoenix had never felt so focused on anything in his life. His concentration never flagged. Not when Mum mentioned Andreas quite unexpectedly over breakfast. Not when Laura questioned him anxiously about the game. He fielded their questions confidently, without once arousing their suspicions. Unbeknown to them, he had the disc, he had the PR suits, he had the will to fight. Nothing fazed him. His mind was on that evening's work: the suit that clung like a second skin, the disc that would open the gate between the worlds, the Angel of Death that would sing for him in battle.

I'm ready.

He did feel a pang of regret as he said goodbye to Laura at the top of her road. She had been with him on that first journey, and she had never been less than brave and resourceful. There was a time when she seemed to belong to the myth-world almost as much as he did. But this was his call. Destiny beckoned him, and him alone. He couldn't afford sentimentality. The stakes were too high. The Gamesmaster was pitiless. In the past he had used the people Phoenix cared about against him. Now it was time to tread the darkness alone. He glanced at his watch. 3.30 p.m. All the time in the world to lay everything out, to prepare himself, then to enter the game. But a shock awaited him when he let himself into the house.

'Dad!' Panic ripped through him. His plans were unravelling in front of him.

'Hello Phoenix.'

Phoenix was suddenly very aware of the Angel of Death hanging behind the chest of drawers, the disc under the floorboards, the darkening of the sky and the imminence of the full moon. 'But what are you doing back so early?'

'I've been waiting for you. I found something out today. About Chris Darke. It confirmed what we've both suspected.' Time was ticking by. Time that was precious. 'That stuff about a cult slaying. I finally managed to speak to the reporter who wrote the piece for the local rag. She took some persuading, but I eventually got her to spill the beans. Off the record, of course.'

Why didn't Dad just get to the point?

'There were puncture marks on his neck, Phoenix. Chris Drake had been bitten. Not by an animal. This was savagery beyond belief, deep, fatal gashes that gouged right into his shoulder. His body was completely drained of blood.'

Phoenix had barely listened until then. He'd been willing Dad out of the door so that he could make himself ready. But this!

'A vampire bite?'

'Looks like it. Of course the police have it down as the work of a madman. How could they imagine anything else?'

Phoenix was thrown into confusion. 'But how can that be? The demons can't break through. If they could, it would all be over by now.'

'I've been asking myself the same question, Phoenix. All I can tell you are the facts. Chris Darke was found dead in his own house, killed by a vampire bite.'

Phoenix could feel his pulse racing, the blood hammering in his head.

'You've got to be careful, Phoenix. The killer might come here.'

'Why would he?'

Dad looked flustered. He wasn't going to tell Phoenix he had the disc.

And I'm not telling you that you don't!

'I don't know, but if he were to come, just get out.'

'Don't worry Dad, I will.'

All the while they had been speaking, John Graves had been as jumpy as his son. 'Just be careful.' Dad glanced at his watch. 'I've got to get back to work. I've got a meeting at five. If I hit the motorway before the rush hour, I ought to just make it back in time.'

'But why did you go to all the trouble of coming home? Why didn't you just phone me?'

Dad shook his head. 'I had to tell you face to face. You were right. This isn't over, not by a long chalk. I'll see you tonight, then.'

'Sure, tonight.'

But you won't see me tonight. By then I will be gone.

To another world.

Phoenix watched Dad accelerating away down the road. He stood at the window a while, allowing his heartbeat to return to normal. It was time. There was no going back.

11

Laura was in a lousy mood. She'd forgotten her maths textbook and had had to run all the way back to school. She had had to almost beg Mr Owen, the caretaker, to let her in. Now, almost an hour late, she heard footsteps behind her, then a boy's voice calling her name. She turned.

'Phoenix? I thought you'd gone home ages ago.' Her smile vanished the moment she looked back. The road behind her was quite empty. 'Phoenix?' She wasn't imagining it. She had heard footsteps right behind her, familiar ones. Phoenix playing tricks. It had to be. He'd often waited around for her like this.

'Phoenix,' she repeated, 'This isn't funny. Come out.' Nervousness crept into her voice. Was it Phoenix? It wasn't like him to carry a joke on this long. He wasn't like other boys. Teasing wasn't in his nature. He was serious, loyal. It was while she was looking down the road, peering through the slight evening haze, that she heard the footsteps again. She knew now that, whoever it was, it wasn't Phoenix. He wouldn't do that. He wouldn't circle her the way a predator stalks its victim.

'Who's there?'

She wasn't a confident teenager any more. Here, on the lonely street, she became a little girl again, unsettled by the nameless menace around her. Fright was rippling over her skin. She was paralysed, scared to stand still, terrified of turning round.

'Why are you doing this? It isn't fair.'

Then it happened. Something brushed against her, barely making contact, but it was enough to make her gag on her own terror. A scream fought to escape from her throat, then clogged and died. She couldn't run, she couldn't scream.

'Who are you?' Those were her words, but the thought that was in her mind was:

What are you?

Pull yourself together, girl, she thought, you've been scared before. And by worse than this. But the presence was powerful. A raw, vengeful, pent-up power was there. Something familiar, but transformed. Something ordinary, yet alien.

You won't be weak, Laura, she told herself. You're going to run. That's the top of your street over there. You're going to turn and you're going to run. On the count of three.

Run! Before she could go even a few strides, her way was blocked. By a youth.

But more than a youth. A teenage boy whose lips drew back in a sneer, whose eyes flashed blood-red in the oncoming night, whose body seemed to blot out the milky whiteness of the rising moon.

Her heart went limp in her chest. Despair filled every fibre of her being.

'You!'

12

Phoenix didn't feel Laura's terror. He didn't hear her muffled scream or the scrape of her shoes as she was dragged away. He had work to do. He hurried to his room and took his rucksack from the top of the wardrobe. He felt around. Already inside were the things he'd bought for his mission: a mallet, steel tent pegs, strong line for sea fishing, several high-power torches. Fastening a utility belt purchased from the local DIY shop round his waist, he loaded the pouches. Before pulling his long top over the belt, he inserted the final item in his armoury, a small hatchet he had found in the garage. It was still as good as new. Phoenix quickly packed the result of his work over the previous few days. The sharpened stakes, the bolts, finally the Angel of Death itself. It was only as he turned to go that he became aware of the chill in the room.

'But I didn't leave a gale blowing through it like this.' The hairs twitched at the back of his neck. He stared at the wide open window. Phoenix flew to the loose floorboard where he had hidden the disc. Still there. Next he checked the room for evidence of a search. Nothing was disturbed. Everything was as it ought to be.

Everything except the window. 'Oh, snap out of it. Everything's here.' His sense of mission took over again. Slipping the rucksack over one shoulder, he ran to the study. Depositing the heavy backpack on the computer table, he pulled the PR suit from the box. Daylight was fading. The afterglow of the sun was a blood-red stain on the clouds. He slipped on the suit. That's when the first anxiety came. He couldn't help himself.

Experiencing that sliding closeness, the way the material seemed to grow into his skin, fuse with it, he felt fear flooding through him.

Keep your nerve, Phoenix. Now of all times.

He reached for the face mask that completed the suit. He was about to attach it to the suit when he made the discovery.

The second suit was gone!

He put his hand into the box. No doubt about it. This time he wasn't just afraid. He was filled with hopeless, gut-melting horror. This wasn't, this couldn't be Dad. Phoenix's nerves jangled. The window, the missing suit. What was happening?

Then came the moonglow. The dark seemed to fall back in awe of the full moon. 'No time to think about this now. I have to act. Before it's too late.' Pulling the mask tight over his face, he closed the last fastening and plugged the suit into the computer. While the disc was downloading, he pulled on the rucksack and waited. He watched the screen clearing and the first images of the game starting to flicker across it. But the evening wasn't done with its surprises yet. When it came to the game, everything came in threes.

First the window, then the suit, now . . . the message on the screen. Phoenix reeled as if under an axe blow.

A single word repeated. A stupid catchphrase that had become a byword for danger and betrayal.

Surprise surprise.

'Adams!'

My enemy. My nemesis.

Phoenix instinctively reached for the lead that linked the suit to the computer. Something was terribly wrong. There was still time to yank it out, time to call the whole thing off. His fingers closed round the lead, then just as quickly released it.

'No, I won't back out. So what if you're waiting for me?' As the golden light began to spiral out of the computer, shimmering with myriads of numbers – threes, sixes, nines – he clenched his fists. He squeezed until his nails were almost gouging his flesh through the thin material.

'I will fight you!' he cried. 'Fight you all!' For a moment the entire study was suffused with pulsating light then, without a sound, the brightness died.

Phoenix was gone.

BOOK TWO

___

The Book of Sight

1

Bird's Eye could feel his heart hammering, his skin tingling with fright. Then the crawling sensation was right inside him, setting off the panicky rat-a-tat-tatting of his heart. It was there in front of him and his mother. Tall as a man, but possessing infinitely more power, its steel-hard spine arched, its jaws bared, dripping blood and thick, viscous saliva.

The night-killer.

Wolver.

'Your crossbow?'

'Tom took it.'

Mum's face was set, her lips pinched into a thin, almost white line. 'I've got the revolver,' she hissed. 'But there are only two shots left.'

Bird's Eyed knew they wouldn't be enough. He had seen enough rippers to know they could take five, six or even more shots and continue their attack almost without interruption. The Wolver radiated menace. It was a giant; a grey, walking nightmare.

'Get behind me, darling. I'll try to hold him off to cover your escape.'

'No,' said Bird's Eye, 'I won't leave you.'

'You must! There is no sense in us both dying on this street.'

'I won't go!'

The Wolver paced from side to side, fire-red eyes piercing the night.

'Stinking hell-fiend,' snarled Bird's Eye. 'What's it waiting for?' Something rustled in the bushes. Bird's Eye felt his breath ball up inside his throat.

'Sucker,' whispered Mum, as the creature emerged from the mansion house garden. It had somehow survived Captain Lawrence's dynamite. Just. One taloned arm had been ripped away completely, leaving the shoulder socket exposed. White bone, grey flesh, dark blood. Its hideous face had been shredded by shrapnel and glass fragments. One eye was reduced to a mess of thick, tar-black Vampyr gore. But its murderous apparatus of attack was still intact. Razor talons, gleaming fangs.

'Sweet heavens!' gasped Ann, revolted by the spectacle.

Bird's Eye met her gaze. He knew what she was thinking. There was only one way to save them both from an appalling death. The revolver. It had two bullets in the chamber.

One for the mother. One for the son.

'Do it,' Bird's Eye told her in a voice that was firm, but stripped of hope. With the ripper and the sucker closing, Ann pressed the gun to his temple. He closed his eyes.

'No!' A strong yet youthful voice whipcracked through the evening air. 'Hit the ground!'

It was an unfamiliar command, but the Van Helsings got the drift, hurling themselves full-length on the pavement. Bird's Eye heard quick, agile footsteps as the newcomer raced across the road. A second sound followed immediately, that of the Wolver's powerful frame thudding onto the cobbled carriage-way. Bird's Eye saw a crossbow bolt sticking out of the beast's breast. The quarrel had pierced the ripper's heart.

The one-armed Vampyr stopped to examine the Wolver. There was no sympathy, only curiosity. Then the sucker locked onto the stranger, hissing and snarling its hatred. As the sucker prepared to attack, Ann raised her revolver and pumped both bullets into it. The Vampyr clutched its rib cage, watching the black blood oozing through its long, clawed fingers.

Then it leered.

It was a gesture of contempt. It tensed and hurled itself at

Ann. Instinctively, she flung an arm in front of her face, but the death-lunge never came. The sucker was down, a crossbow bolt sticking out of its side.

'Mother!' Bird's Eye yelled. 'I see another. The one who was missing from the cellar.' They'd wondered about the absence of the brood-master. 'A master Vampyr.'

'Run!' the stranger ordered. 'Get away from here.' The Van Helsings hesitated. 'I'm loaded and you're unarmed. Leave me to handle it. Go that way. Wait for me down by the river.'

Ann examined the adolescent boy who was giving orders with such remarkable authority. His manner, his speech, the cut of his hair, they all looked strange. But where was he from? She thought she had met all the Committee's European contacts. How could so adept a hunter be unknown to her? And how old was he? Fifteen, sixteen?

'We can't . . .'

'Please don't argue. Just go. I'll follow in a few minutes.'

2

Phoenix looked along the deserted street, first to the left then to the right. Bird's Eye had mentioned a Vampyr, a master. So where was it? Brandishing the Angel of Death, Phoenix poked the bolt into the bushes that overhung the garden wall. He glimpsed the scorched, shattered wall where the dynamite had gone off. Everything was still. There was no sign of movement anywhere. He was seeing things.

Taking advantage of the respite, Phoenix edged over to the Wolver. Gingerly, he knelt down and pulled the bolt from its side. Time to recover the tools of his trade. Wiping the blood off on its fur, he slipped the bolt back into the makeshift quiver in his belt. He glanced at his wrist, noting the score he had already built up on his points bracelet.

As if it were a game.

For a moment, Phoenix marvelled at his own composure. It was a feeling he had had in his first adventure. Not helplessness, not oppression, but a contradictory stew of terror and exhilaration. He had thrown off his own world as if it were an old coat, too tight, too worn, too familiar.

I'm born to this.

But the rules of the game had changed since that first foray into a myth-world. The Gamesmaster had dispensed with most of the trappings of the game. There were the points, but could he trust them? Might they not be just one of the Gamesmaster's deceptions? The demon-lord had stripped the game down but Phoenix was ready. He was continuing to retrieve his bolts for round two. Ruthless efficiency would be his strategy from then on. 'Now for the one I put into you, Mr Vampyr.' Phoenix's eyes scanned the street nervously as he knelt and tugged at the second bolt. This one was tougher to shift. 'Come out.'

That's what it happened. The Vampyr's unmutilated eye opened, making Phoenix's words die in his throat. With a hiss like water on a red hot hob, the sucker sprang, surging up like lightning, dashing the crossbow from Phoenix's hand.

The quarrel couldn't have pierced its heart. Why didn't I check?

Using his left hand to fend off the Vampyr, Phoenix felt for his hatchet with his right. But one hand was never going to be enough to stay the demon's frenzied assault. A spasm of pain jolted through Phoenix. The Vampyr's talons slashed at him, its blood-red eyes staring into his. It came at him, a scything of claws, a lunging of teeth. Phoenix thought he had got himself ready, but nothing could have prepared him for this. He saw the colourless lips draw back, revealing lethal fangs.

'No!'

He was squirming and flailing, fighting for his life. The points score was tumbling. Even with only one arm the creature was too strong for him. Phoenix could feel his strength draining away, but with one last effort he managed to yank the hatchet out of his belt and smash it into the Vampyr's chest. He felt its body rock, the honed edge of the axe-head crunching bone and cartilage, but its grip on him didn't ease even one tenth. Phoenix felt hope seeping out of him.

Csssss!

The Vampyr's mouldering face was so close, Phoenix was assaulted by the oily smell of death. Rotten-sweet, the stench of decay was almost overpowering.

'Get it over with then,' yelled Phoenix, feeling the hatchet bouncing harmlessly off his assailant's rotting, maggoty chest. But instead of completing the kill, the sucker loosened its grip on him and stepped back.

65

Why?

Two words provided the answer. 'Surprise surprise.'

Phoenix went cold. Adams. And then he saw her. 'Laura!' Adams was holding her by the hair, wrenching her head back brutally. 'So that's why you took the PR suit,' said Phoenix. 'To transport Laura into this hell, to use her against me.' Then a frown came over his face. 'But you didn't need to take it from the study,' he said grimly. 'You didn't need to come to the house at all. The Gamesmaster's factory is mass-producing them ready for the launch. Why take it from under my nose? Why leave that message?'

Then came the realization. 'You wanted to boast, didn't you? That's it, you wanted me crushed, you wanted to tell me you'd won.' He glanced at the points bracelet. His score was low, but it was still above survival level. 'Well, you haven't. I'll never give up.'

Adams affected a yawn. 'I'm not surprised you found your way through the gateway,' he said. 'My master expected as much. In fact, we welcome it.' He twisted his fingers through Laura's hair, making her cry out.

'Leave her alone,' warned Phoenix. 'If you want to fight somebody, fight me. I've beaten you before and I'll do it again.' He was trying to sound confident, but his heart had dropped through a trap door. There was something different about Adams. Phoenix couldn't believe how he had changed. The features were still those of the fourteen year old boy who had been his rival at school, but he looked taller, more powerfully built. His face was set into a mould of savagery. He was wearing a tunic that harked back to former times. He was dressed all in black, his jacket studded with iron.

'How long is it since we met last?' asked Adams.

'Six weeks.'

'Six short weeks,' sighed Adams. 'You won't imagine what I've seen, what I've done.'

Phoenix gave him a suspicious stare.

'You don't believe me, do you?' said Adams. 'So tell me,

how do you think I got like this?' He roared with laughter. That's when Phoenix saw the fangs.

'You're one of them!' he cried, his skin clammy with fright.

'A Vampyr? Why yes, so I am, for the purposes of this game. Not just any old Vampyr either, I am master of my brood.'

'Are you all right, Laura?' asked Phoenix, ignoring Adams' boasting.

'Well,' said Adams, relaxing his hold on her slightly. 'Aren't you going to answer him?'

Laura fixed him with a look made in equal parts of terror and contempt, then shouted, 'Run Phoenix. Save yourself!'

'Do you know,' Adams sneered into her face, 'I don't think your little playmate's going anywhere.'

The one-armed Vampyr had moved behind Phoenix, blocking his escape. It was unnecessary, Phoenix had no intention of fleeing. 'What do you want, Adams?'

'What do you think? On this, the first day of renewed hostilities, I will accept nothing less than unconditional surrender. A first step towards my master's rising.'

'You think I'm going to stand by while you get the game into every home. Think I'll give in and abandon the world to the demons? You don't know me very well, do you Adams? You can drop dead.'

Adams tapped his fangs and brandished his claws. 'Sorry,' he said, engaging in a show of gallows humour. 'But in a sense I already did that.' He chuckled at his own joke, then forced Laura to her knees. His talons pinched her flesh. The school bully had evolved into something that was barely human. 'What does it take to get some sense out of you, Phoenix? Maybe I should feed sweet Laura to our friend.'

The one-armed Vampyr looked interested, cocking its mutilated head and coming closer to Laura.

'Leave her alone,' snapped Phoenix.

Adams tutted. 'You're not in a position to give me orders.' Adams' voice had changed, filling with a low thunder. This too was new, true evil replacing the mischief of old. 'I don't think so, Phoenix. I've chosen my path, and my mentor. I left Brownleigh and our playground scuffles behind long ago. You will find that I have undergone a complete transformation, and I adore the new me. I think it's time you grovelled. That way, I may make the end merciful.'

He brandished his blade-like talons. 'One slash and I will open her throat from ear to ear. Now what have you got to say for yourself?'

'Don't touch her . . .'

'Oh, what next?' drawled Adams. 'You're so predictable. How does the speech go? *Lay a hand on her and I'll never rest until I make you pay.* You've watched too many movies, Phoenix. Well, forget it. This is the real world. The good guys don't have to win. Back in the old world I would have to face the consequences of my actions. Here . . .'

He spread his arms. 'Here I can do exactly as I wish, without fear of retribution. Hear that, I can do what I like. Don't believe me? Then watch.' His clawed hand stroked Laura's cheek, then ran slowly down her throat. A drop of blood oozed from the first slight nick he cut into her neck. The one-armed Vampyr moved in, intoxicated by the scent. It was thirsting after her. It wanted to feed. 'See how he looks at her, Phoenix, that wild, savage craving. Think I should give him a little taste? Just enough to make her one of us.'

'Get off her!'

It wasn't Phoenix's words which stopped Adams in his track, but a crossbow bolt that drilled itself right through his clawed hand. The bolt jolted Adams back, pinning his hand to the wall.

'Laura, run!'

She didn't need telling twice. Struggling free, she raced towards Phoenix, shouting a warning. 'Behind you,' she screamed.

Phoenix's eyes had been drawn to Adams squirming on the arrow. He had forgotten the one-armed Vampyr. Seeing Ann

68

Van Helsing wielding the Angel of Death, he appealed for help.
'Shoot!'

'No bolts,' cried Ann. 'I've just shot the one you left primed.'

Phoenix squeezed the handle of the hatchet. It slid in his grip.

Strength, don't fail me now.

He swung the axe with all his might into the Vampyr's face, taking its remaining eye and splitting open its skull. Bone crunched and jelly burst, black blood spilling into its evil mouth. Phoenix had recovered his will to win. Sheathing the hatchet he produced mallet and tent pin and hammered the pin into the sucker's heart. He felt skin and bone pop and heard the sickening gurgle in its throat. He drove it in hard and true, leaving no room for error. As he drew back, he wondered at his own ruthlessness. He was standing panting over the dead Vampyr when Laura shouted again.

'Phoenix, look . . .'

Adams had wrenched his hand from the wall and was slowly drawing the bolt, a shriek of pain bursting from his lungs. Phoenix raced across the road and snatched the Angel from Ann. Within seconds he had loaded and fired the quarrel, the bolt thudding into Adams' shoulder, doubling his agony.

'Now move,' Phoenix ordered, leading Laura and the Van Helsings from the scene.

3

'What made you come back?' panted Phoenix, quickly glancing behind for some sign of Adams.

'I saw the suckers,' Bird's Eye explained. 'The master and the legionary.'

'Saw them? How?'

Ann smiled indulgently. 'He doesn't mean see with his eyes. With his mind. Robert has a second sight. He has possessed it from infancy. He would be sitting in his playpen up in the nursery and I'd hear him say: *Grandfather*. Moments later there would be my father's familiar rap at the door. When he was six or seven, he once burst into tears. He claimed to have witnessed an old horse crumple and die on the road. I thought it was just his imagination. Days later I was to discover that the incident had occurred several miles away, something he couldn't have known about any other way.'

'I see the way a bird sees,' Bird's Eye explained. 'It's as if I'm up there, gliding on the air currents.'

'Hence the nickname Bird's Eye,' said Ann.

'Only I don't see things sharply,' Bird's Eye continued. 'They're not pictures. I see the shadows of things. I have to read them correctly. It's something I'm getting better at as I get older.' Phoenix felt something stirring inside him, a deep unease, and he knew better than to dismiss his instincts.

'OK,' he said dubiously. 'So if you're as good as you say, what's at the end of this alleyway?'

'It doesn't work like that,' said Bird's Eye. 'I don't choose the sight. It chooses me.'

Phoenix gave Robert Van Helsing another long, appraising look. 'We've got to get off the streets,' he said. 'I think I've only slowed Adams down.'

Ann nodded. 'Follow me. We will take the omnibus to Limehouse. I know of lodgings there, somewhere we will not be traced. The rooms are modest, but the landlady is a friend of the Committee. We will be safe there.'

Phoenix gave the street a final inspection. It seemed unlikely that they would be safe anywhere.

The omnibus ride was an uncomfortable affair. Uncomfortable because of the poorly upholstered seats. Uncomfortable because of the stares they were attracting. The game had transformed their clothes, but it couldn't do much with the colour of Laura's skin or her beaded locks. Phoenix looked out on to the streets of this unfamiliar London, a city at the crossroads between the nineteenth and twentieth centuries. The petrol-engined cars, taxis and buses vied with horse-drawn cabs and hansoms for every inch of bustling roadway.

'You went without me,' Laura whispered, more than a trace of accusation in her voice. 'Have I done something wrong?'

Phoenix glanced at the Van Helsings. 'It's not that I don't trust you,' he said. 'You know better than that. I didn't want you being used against me.'

'The way Adams used me, you mean?'

Phoenix gave a half-smile. 'He was a step ahead of me, wasn't he?'

'It isn't the old Adams. What's happened to him?'

Phoenix shook his head. 'I don't know. He was always a nasty piece of work, but nothing like this. I thought he was a bit of a buffoon really. I don't think I was ever actually scared of him. Now . . .' He remembered the curved fangs, the glinting talons. What was human in Adams seemed to have all but fallen away, leaving only the kernel of wickedness. '. . . I don't know.'

They were interrupted by a breezy shout from the conductor. 'Inkerman Street. All passengers for Inkerman Street.'

A pack of ragged boys tumbled down the stairs from the upper deck, laughing and hitting one another with their caps. Two old workmen grumbled and tutted and scraped their hobnailed boots on the floor. Ann leaned forward and tapped Phoenix on the shoulder.

'This is where we get off.'

Number nine, Inkerman Street, wasn't the flop house Phoenix had been expecting. It was a clean, well-kept, if sparsely furnished rooming house. The landlady, Mrs Cave, greeted Ann with an embrace and a kiss on the cheek. 'My dear,' she said warmly. 'I'm so glad to see you here.'

'Alive, you mean?' said Ann.

'And you, my dear Robert,' Mrs Cave continued. 'You're growing into such a fine, handsome young man.' She tousled his blond hair, and led them into a large kitchen. She stood with her back to the black-leaded range. Ann took a chair beside her.

'Are there any other lodgers this evening?'

'No, we are quite alone here.'

'Good.'

'I feared for you, Ann,' said Mrs Cave. 'After the dreadful news about poor Mr Bloch.'

Ann saw Phoenix's querying look. 'Bloch was the seventh member of the Committee to die,' Ann explained. 'You do know about the Committee?'

'I can make an educated guess,' said Phoenix.

'The Committee has been coordinating our efforts to resist this Vampyr plague,' Ann told him. 'At first we had our successes, but in the last few months we have suffered reverse after reverse. More and more nests of suckers, fewer and fewer fighters to destroy them. It has been dreadful, Mr . . .'

'My name is Phoenix Graves. This is Laura Osibona. First names will do.'

'Well, Phoenix,' she began, hesitating over the curious name, 'It began with my father, founder of the Committee.'

'Professor Van Helsing was the first man to warn of the Vampyr plague,' Mrs Cave interrupted. 'A great man.'

'He was ambushed and killed in central Europe. He died in Dracul's lair.'

'Dracul?'

'Lord of Vampyrs. Progenitor of the evil host. After Father's death, everything seemed to crumble. One after another, the leaders of our society fell, and all the while the Legion of demons grew in power. You find us at a low ebb, I'm afraid. But enough of us, how did you come to join the cause?'

Phoenix drew up a chair. 'You promise you will hear me out?' he asked. 'Even if what I have to say flies in the face of everything you believe to be true?'

At the end of the telling, Ann Van Helsing glanced at her son. 'Robert?'

Bird's Eye closed his eyes. For a few moments he appeared to be resting. When he reopened his eyes, he looked dazed. 'I think he is telling the truth,' he told her. 'Even now we are being watched. It is as though we are trapped, being controlled almost.' There was truth in Bird's Eye's vision. A world away, an anguished John and Christina Graves were watching their son's progress on the monitor in the study. All around them, the world was caught in freeze-frame. There was only one time now; the game's time.

'That's the computer,' said Phoenix. 'It's the gateway from my world into yours.'

Ann stood up and paced the tiled floor. 'Even that is not the most difficult thing to accept,' she said. 'From girlhood, I have accompanied my father into all kinds of crypts and castles. I have seen wraiths and ghouls and the shape-shifting creatures of the night. I have seen Hell in all its manifestations. It is but a short step to believe in other worlds. What I am unable to accept is that all of us here . . .' She indicated Mrs Cave and Bird's Eye. '. . . and all our comrades are unwitting pawns in some demon-lord's plan. Are you really trying to tell us that all this, our entire world, is a mere game and that we are a monster's playthings?'

'What would that make us?' Mrs Cave protested, 'Rows of clockwork toys waiting to be wound up? You insult us.'

'No,' said Phoenix, 'I'm not saying that.' He took a deep breath. 'Look, I'm sure that even here, in a myth-world, people can choose their own path. They *can* fight the Gamesmaster as you are doing. If that were not true, then everything truly would be lost.' He looked directly at the Van Helsings. 'What I am telling you is that he is always in the shadows, manipulating you. He aims to rule all worlds. Yours, mine and whatever other worlds lie out there, as yet undiscovered. And if you really want to know why you have lost so many of your comrades, it is because he has outwitted you all the way. Believe me, I have seen it before. Within your ranks, there may be people who, whether knowingly or not, act on behalf of the Gamesmaster. That is how he gains control. It is not only the horror, though that is real enough. He can control minds, twist thoughts, make people dance like puppets. Your world already dances to his tune. I won't let mine go the same way.'

Ann reeled at the revelation. 'Traitors! My father, all my friends were sacrificed by traitors?'

Mrs Cave started up from her chair. 'It's not true!' she cried indignantly. 'No, I won't have it. It beggars belief.' She turned on Phoenix. 'How do you know he can be trusted, Ann? What do you know about him? There were no traitors in our society. It is an insult to the men and woman who have given up everything in its service. Who could have known enough to destroy the organization? Only the Committee of Nine itself! With the exception of yourself, Ann, and one other, they are all dead.'

Mrs Cave built herself up for one last rebuttal. 'Are you pointing the finger at Ann, or at dead men?' she demanded. 'No Sir, there are no traitors. Unless, that is, you are the one the demon-lord has sent.'

74

4

The lights were still burning in Mrs Cave's lodging house at three in the morning. Though the gas lamps were turned down to afford some rest to tired eyes, nobody thought of climbing the stairs to bed. The cause of their restless vigil was Bird's Eye's sudden declaration:

'Evil is awake this night.'

Once dusk began to gather and shadows stole down the alleyways outside, Bird's Eye had been overwhelmed by a sense of foreboding. Evil was awake, and it had its eyes open. It was watching them, waiting to strike.

'What's that?' asked Laura, during one of the many lulls in conversation. All eyes turned in her direction.

'I didn't hear anything,' said Phoenix.

'And I didn't see anything,' said Bird's Eye.

Laura resumed her seat, knowing that her words didn't carry the same weight as Bird's Eye's. 'Sorry,' she said. 'Jumpy, I suppose. Maybe they just won't come.'

'They'll come,' said Ann. 'I trust my son's insights.'

Suddenly, Laura shot bolt upright, knocking her chair over. Everybody started. 'There it is again,' she said, eyes round. 'I'm not imagining it. I did hear something. Why can't any of you hear it?'

Phoenix cocked his ear. Outside in the darkness there was a scraping, crackling sound. 'Laura's right.'

Mrs Cave frowned. 'Well, I can't hear anything,' she said dismissively.

Phoenix disagreed. 'There is something. I'll . . .'

Nobody got to know what he meant to say next. At that very moment the back and front doors of number nine Inkerman Street were smashed in simultaneously, splinters of wood and metal fittings flying everywhere. The crash of the doors was accompanied by a nerve-shredding cacophony of shrieking and snarling.

'Arm yourselves!' Ann screamed.

Mrs Cave had provided a well-stocked arsenal. The deadly apparatus had been laid out ready. In the space of a few seconds, everyone was armed with a crossbow. Stakes, mallets and a pair of pistols also lay on the table, ready for use. They moved quickly to their places, following a rough sort of plan.

Ann and Bird's Eye were standing either side of the door which opened onto the hallway. Laura and Mrs Cave were kneeling behind the overturned table, using it as an impromptu barricade as they covered the back way. Phoenix chose not to join either position. Instead, he reserved the right to act according to his instincts. He stood in the middle of the floor, looking down the hallway. That's when he saw the first Vampyr. Its bleached, high-domed head was quite hairless. Its eyes were dark red points among the multiple folds of its wrinkled face. Its thin, colourless lips were drawn back to reveal stiletto-thin, razor-sharp fangs. As it advanced, he shot his first bolt directly into its chest. He knew before it hit the floor that it was dead. But one kill was never going to halt the Vampyr assault. The Legion cared nothing for its casualties, only for their master's victory.

'More this way!' yelled Laura.

They were pouring in through the scullery window, swarming towards their prey. Three of them. Laura got the leader, but as she tried to reload, she screamed. Danger had come from an unexpected source. Mrs Cave had pinned her arms and was pushing her towards the Vampyrs.

'Take her!' the old woman shrieked.

'Are you insane?' cried Laura. 'What are you doing?'

The sucker came on, making wide, scything movements with its arm.

'Get your head down!' shouted Phoenix as he sent a bolt thudding into the Vampyr's chest. Laura dug her elbow into Mrs Cave's stomach. Hearing a gasp of pain, she wriggled free and fled across the room. Phoenix, having quickly reloaded, dispatched the final Vampyr, then turned on Mrs Cave. 'You're one of them.'

Mrs Cave just laughed, flaunting her defiance. 'I serve a greater cause.' They were the last words she spoke. Ann Van Helsing turned and shot a bolt into her heart.

'She was a Vampyr?'

Phoenix shook his head. He bent down and pulled down the woman's high, starched collar, revealing a mark like a tattoo. It was in the shape of a bat. 'She was one of the traitors I told you about. This is the Gamesmaster's brand.' He glanced at Bird's Eye. 'Is the attack over?'

Bird's Eye shook his head. 'I see movement in the street. It's barely even started.' Then his eyes widened. 'They're below us. Get away from the middle of the floor!'

Hardly had the words left his mouth when the floor erupted, tiles spinning everywhere. A Wolver was bursting through from the cellar below their feet. Ann and Bird's Eye hit it in the back and throat with bolts. It howled, but it didn't die. Instead, it twisted round and the ferocious jaws snapped at them.

'Here,' said Phoenix. 'Take her. She's one of you.' He kicked Mrs Cave's body at the Wolver. Seeing the creature tearing the corpse to shreds, Ann pumped three shots into the Wolver's face and Phoenix set about it with the hatchet. The beast howled and bellowed with pain. It was shaking its massive shoulders, tossing what was left of Mrs Cave about like a rag doll. In a flurry of silver-grey fur and snapping jaws, it was gone, dragging the body away.

'What now?' asked Laura.

'We can't stay here,' said Phoenix. 'We'll be trapped inside this house. We've got to break out.'

'Which way?' Ann asked her son.

'The back,' said Bird's Eye.

'Sure?' asked Phoenix. 'I mean, you let those things creep up on us. What happened to the famous sight?'

Bird's Eye turned away. Tears were welling in his eyes. 'I don't know. I predicted their coming, but the attack still took me by surprise. I'm sorry.'

'Sorry?' snapped Phoenix. 'You nearly got us killed. And why didn't you know about Mrs Cave?'

Bird's Eye hung his head.

'Stop it!' shouted Ann. 'Why are you doing this? You're not helping.'

Laura backed her up. 'She's right. Why are you being so horrible?'

Phoenix scowled. If any of them had shared one iota of the suspicions that were crowding his mind, they would be acting in exactly the same fashion. 'Seems funny how this sight of yours conveniently failed when the suckers showed up, don't you think?'

Ann turned away. 'We're going out of the back door. With or without you, Phoenix, I don't really care which.' In the event, they emerged from the house together, hurrying along the back alley and into Sevastopol Street, which branched off Inkerman Street to the left.

'Which way?' asked Laura.

Phoenix held up his hand for quiet. 'I don't think it's over yet.' Sure enough, with a hiss, two Vampyrs dropped from a wall, taking Ann down by their weight alone, slamming her face on the pavement.

'Bird's Eye,' Phoenix yelled. 'Get out of the way. I can't get a shot.' The Vampyrs had Ann pinned and helpless. One was wrestling her over on to her back. The other was craning forward, its leering jaws seeking her throat. Still Bird's Eye stood rooted to the spot.

'Move!'

But he was frozen in horror, staring at the struggle in front of him. In the end, Phoenix had no choice but to barge him out of the way. He killed the first Vampyr with a single shot.

'Phoenix!' Laura handed him her bow and he released the trigger. He heard the punching crack of the bolt, but he didn't manage a clean kill. The sucker jolted into the air, and Phoenix saw it coming at him in a rage of pain and hatred. He wanted it slain, wiped out, annihilated, but he was disarmed. The Vampyr struck him a painful blow in the chest, winding him. Phoenix spun round, crumpling under the impact. As he crashed to the ground, the Angel of Death fell from his grip. The demon had him by the collar of his jacket. It was dragging him to his feet. Then he felt a spasm run through its body. Laura had grabbed Ann's gun and pumped two shots into it. Still it didn't let go. Phoenix saw the fangs flash and closed his eyes. He could feel the points bracelet throbbing on his wrist. He knew his score was in free fall. That's when the creature shuddered one last time and finally tumbled to the pavement.

Phoenix turned round to express his gratitude to whoever had come to his aid. 'Bird's Eye!'

It was Robert Van Helsing who had shot the decisive quarrel.

5

It was dawn before they were able to sleep, but when they did it was in spacious rooms, the daylight shut out by heavy, velvet curtains. At last they were safe. Vampyrs stalked the night. Come daybreak, they had to seek the shadows. Sunlight would turn them to ash. Phoenix stretched out on the crisp white sheets and smiled with sheer pleasure in the comfortable bed. Since the attack on Inkerman Street, Ann had given up her thoughts of hiding in another secret location. It was obvious that their every move was known to their enemy. She took them instead to the large town house of Ramsay Foxton, a friend of her late father. He and Ann were the last two survivors of the Committee of Nine. His house had become its headquarters. It was the thought of the Committee of Nine that wiped the smile from Phoenix's face.

Seven dead.

He frowned. Almost the entire leadership of the movement had been wiped out. Resistance to the Legion was hanging by a thread. Phoenix knew that Mrs Cave wasn't operating on her own. The Gamesmaster had to have more pawns working for him. But who were they? Phoenix lay back, allowing the images that had been troubling him to swirl around in his head. Adams was there, the Van Helsings, Mum and Dad and finally a man he had never met, but who may have had the greatest bearing on his destiny . . . Andreas.

Phoenix was woken some six hours later by a knock on the door. 'Yes?'

'There is a hot meal downstairs in the dining room,' said a female voice. 'Given the lateness of the hour, I hesitate to call it breakfast, Sir.'

'Why, what time is it?'

'Just before midday.'

'Thank you.'

Phoenix washed, dressed in the Norfolk jacket and flannels that had been laid out for him, and jogged downstairs, marvelling at the opulent surroundings. The meal was served in a large room with damask curtains. In addition to the long, polished oak table, there were armchairs, a sideboard and a piano. The Van Helsings featured prominently among the photographs that crowded every surface.

'Young Mr Graves,' said a silver-haired, bearded man in a wheelchair. 'I was unable to greet you last night, or should I say earlier this morning? I trust my staff looked after your needs.' Phoenix noticed the people who had admitted them on their arrival.

'Yes, thank you.'

Five minutes later, Laura and the Van Helsings joined them. While the four of them ate toast, bacon, eggs and roast potatoes, Foxton sipped lemon tea.

'Ann tells me you have an interesting story to tell, Mr Graves.'

'Call me Phoenix.'

'You believe the threat of Vampyrism is not confined to this world, Phoenix?'

'The power that threatens us goes far beyond Vampyrs,' said Phoenix, exchanging glances with Laura. 'Our enemy counts as his allies all the nightmares that have ever haunted the human mind.'

'And you believe Mrs Cave was just the tip of the iceberg?' asked a burly man who had been listening from across the room. 'Our society is penetrated by traitors?'

'This is Bradshaw,' said Foxton, 'Without his efforts, none of us would be here today.'

'I know that the Gamesmaster has been a step ahead of you for a long time,' said Phoenix, glancing from Bradshaw to Foxton.

Foxton stroked his beard. 'Given the scale of our losses, that seems plausible. The question is, Phoenix, can you finger our traitors?'

'This is my second day in your world, Mr Foxton. I will need time to understand how it works. In fact, I would be grateful if you would tell me what you know about the Vampyrs.'

Foxton glanced at Ann. 'You have here in front of you, Phoenix, our country's two foremost experts on the creature. I was a friend of Professor Van Helsing. You *are* acquainted with the professor's reputation?'

'He fought vampires.'

'He was *the* Vampyr-hunter. It was in an encounter with the hell-fiends in Transylvania five years ago that I lost the use of my legs, and the companionship of the greatest man I ever met. What do you want to know?'

'Everything.'

'From what you have said already, may I take it that there are Vampyr stories in your world too, Phoenix?'

Phoenix nodded.

'Black capes, garlic, crosses?'

'Yes, that's about it.'

'Then dismiss from your mind all that you have heard. You wish to know about the real Vampyr? It doesn't wear a black cloak. It is not afraid of garlic or running water, nor of crosses or priests of any description. Look in a mirror and you will see its face. Nor is it the tragic figure some popular fiction would have us believe. It doesn't have a conscience and it doesn't mourn past loves. There is nothing about it that is sympathetic or human in the slightest. Its heart is stone cold and utterly devoid of feeling. It is a predator's heart. It ticks like a clock and when your time is up, it kills without sentiment or hesitation. It slaughters its prey by tearing open its victim's throat, or by its bite which injects a sickness that causes a slow, agonizing death. Worst of all, it can transform the poor wretch into one of its own kind.'

Laura shuddered.

'The myth of the Vampyr is common to all cultures. The Babylonians, the ancient Greeks and Romans, the peoples of Africa and central Europe all have their Vampyrs. The Indonesians have the Puntianak, India the Vampir and Ireland the Dearg-dul or red blood sucker. It is, my dear Phoenix, a universal horror. The lord of all Vampyrs is Dracul. From his lair in Transylvania, his evil is beginning to reach out across the globe. He has welded these creatures of the night into a single force, the Vampyr Legion. As a result, the Vampyr we face is not the single, solitary, haunted figure you may have read about in some gothic tale. He is part of a vast army, an unthinking footsoldier of the Legion of the Undead which multiplies every day. As if that were not enough to contend with, Dracul employs a regiment of werewolves. The Wolver is a battering-ram. The moon-born beast can smash through a brick wall, demolish it in a trice. Its jaws are like mantraps. These are our foes, my young friend. They are as lethal and implacable as Fate, and at the moment we are losing the battle against them.'

'You must not be so pessimistic, Ramsay,' said Ann, interrupting. 'It's been this way before. It may take years, but we will prevail. We must.'

'Yes, my dear,' said Foxton, taking her hand. 'You're right.'

Phoenix listened with rapt attention as Foxton ran on, explaining the history of the Vampyr and of its generations of opponents. Finally, a full thirty minutes later, he spoke.

'Thank you, Mr Foxton. Now I have a sense of how my enemy operates in this world. But believe me, you have to forget this talk of a long battle. There isn't time for that. For the sake of your world and mine we have to destroy them, and destroy them now.' He sensed the magnitude of the task. 'If this is, as you say, an army then we have to take their general. We have to behead this Legion.' He thought of the invisible demon-lord behind the scenes. 'And even destroying Dracul is only the first step. The Legion is nothing compared with the evil that is running them.'

6

It was mid-afternoon that same day when Bradshaw burst into the sitting room.

'News?' asked Foxton.

'Oh, I've got news all right,' said Bradshaw. 'We've discovered the nest. A warehouse in Royal India Street, down by the docks.' The moment he made the announcement, something changed in the Foxton House. The air of dejection and pessimism lifted. It didn't have the atmosphere of a beleaguered fortress any longer.

'We must move quickly,' said Foxton, checking his watch. 'We have only two hours of daylight left. Leave a skeleton force here with me and take everyone you can muster. You must destroy the entire brood.'

'We won't fail,' said Bradshaw. 'We have young Robert's gift of sight to guide us.'

Phoenix looked up. He didn't share Bradshaw's confidence.

The Vampyr-hunters filled a car and a delivery van. The legend *Bell's Pies* was painted on the side of the van. By the time they were in position outside the warehouse, there remained less than an hour of daylight for their grisly task.

'Well?' said Bradshaw, looking in Bird's Eye's direction. 'Is our intelligence correct? How many do you see?'

Bird's Eye shook his head. 'You've been misinformed. I don't see anything. It's an empty building.'

Several of the Vampyr-hunters threw down their weapons in disgust.

'You're sure, Robert?' said Bradshaw. 'Absolutely certain?'

'It's an empty building,' Bird's Eye answered.

'Blast it! The man who gave us this information has never been wrong before. Kelly, Hewitt, come with me. We'll take a look around.'

'Mind if I come too?' asked Phoenix.

Bradshaw looked him up and down, then nodded. 'Aye, tag along if you wish, but there will be nothing to see. Young master Robert has always been completely reliable.'

You weren't at Inkerman Street, thought Phoenix, arming the Angel.

'You'll have no need of that,' chuckled Kelly.

Phoenix returned his look without a smile. Laura joined the group as they made their way to the door. The remaining Vampyr-hunters kept their disgruntled vigil outside.

'Ready?' asked Bradshaw in his Yorkshire drawl. 'Then let's go.'

Kelly raised his sledgehammer to dash off the lock, but Bradshaw stopped him and reached for the door handle. 'You never know.' Sure enough, the door was open. It only increased Phoenix's suspicions. The moment the party were inside they were assailed by a foul odour.

'Suckers have been here, all right,' said Bradshaw, pressing a handkerchief to his face. 'That smell of decay, I'd recognize it anywhere.'

Laura gagged. 'I feel sick.'

'It's strong,' said Bradshaw, leading the way down the wooden stairs to the floor below. 'We must have only just missed them.'

'Are you sure we *have* missed them?' asked Phoenix, every fibre of his being alert to the possibility of betrayal. 'I don't like this.' Bradshaw was about to answer when there was a terrible shriek.

'Sucker!' screamed Laura.

Phoenix alone had his weapon cocked. He was first to react, nailing the fiend to the wall with a crossbow bolt. He waved the Angel under Kelly's nose. 'Still think I don't need it?'

'Hewitt.' Bradshaw commanded urgently, 'Get up those

stairs. Warn the main party.' Hewitt was less than halfway up the staircase when a second Vampyr scuttled across the wall. It climbed the vertical surface as if it were running across the floor. Before Hewitt could reach it, the Vampyr had locked and bolted the outside door. Then there was an explosion of fury. A wall had burst apart, showering everyone with dust, plaster and bits of brick.

'Wolver!'

It tensed and hurled itself at the staircase, shattering it with the sheer force of its leap. Hewitt was thrown from the disintegrating structure.

'Back!' yelled Bradshaw. 'Load your weapons.'

Kelly was trying to drag Hewitt out of the Wolver's way, but Hewitt had fallen heavily and cried out in agony. Suddenly the entire building was echoing with inhuman shrieking and howling as Vampyrs and Wolvers spilled from every doorway, climbed from every grating. The appalling chorus was followed by a gargle of blood. The Wolver had claimed its first victim. It had caught Kelly unawares as he tried to help his friend and ripped out his throat.

'What happened to the boy's sight?' cried Bradshaw despairingly, seeing the creatures gathering in the gloom. 'He said it was empty. He didn't mention anything about rippers or suckers.'

'Or about masters,' came a voice achingly familiar to Phoenix. It was Adams. He stepped forward with a strutting arrogance.

'Surprise surprise,' he said. 'Our little home from home isn't so empty after all.'

Phoenix and Laura looked up. The windows were boarded up to keep out the sunset's rays.

'It's a trap,' said Phoenix, 'It always was.'

Phoenix, Bradshaw and Laura backed away pulling the half-conscious Hewitt with them. They were outnumbered and outwitted. In the tense silence they could hear the main party hammering at the outside door.

'Even if they force the door, it's a thirty-foot drop,' Bradshaw said grimly.

'What do we do?' groaned Laura.

'That's simple,' said Adams. 'Three of you die and Phoenix becomes one of us. Do you understand now? You're going to open the gate for us.'

'Open it, but how can I?'

'Believe me,' said Adams. 'You'll find a way.' He turned briskly on his heel and barked a single word:

'Attack!'

7

'Cover me!' yelled Bradshaw, drawing his revolver and turning to aim it at the windows above their heads. Phoenix and Laura shot their bolts into the crowd of demons and started reloading. In the same instant, Bradshaw shot out a window.

'Don't come through the door,' he cried to the hunters outside. 'The staircase is gone.' His warning didn't come a moment too early. The Vampyr-hunters had just sledge-hammered the door and were shooting a volley of quarrels into the demon ranks. 'Get the ropes from the van,' Bradshaw ordered, pumping shots into a Wolver that had come too close. Phoenix finished it with a bolt into the heart. More bolts showered down from the Vampyr-hunters above, thinning the ranks of the demons. As quickly as they emerged the night-terrors melted away into the dark heart of the warehouse.

Phoenix felt the breath shudder through him. 'That was too close for comfort.'

The main party had now joined them. Bird's Eye was pale and trembling. 'I was so sure,' he said. Ann put her arm round him. She looked as shattered as her son.

'There's no time for this now,' said Bradshaw. 'We have to finish the night-crawlers.' There was a low sigh from the darkness.

'They're down here,' said Phoenix, crouching over a grating.

The faces of Laura, Ann and Bird's Eye were as white as salt, their eyes blue points of terror.

'No matter how often I do this,' Ann said. 'I never get used to it.'

'I know,' said Bradshaw. 'Don't let the act fool you. Neither do I.'

Phoenix followed him down the iron ladder that led to the basement below. He would have chosen to be anywhere in the whole world, anywhere but that dank, infested warehouse. 'Anything?' he asked, peering into the gloom.

'Nothing,' Bradshaw replied. 'Just that appalling smell.'

The others followed. Then the Wolvers came, two huge silver forms detonating out of the darkness. There was a split-second between Phoenix and Bradshaw's bolts. Both hit their mark. The crazed howling echoed through the blackness. After that . . . silence.

'Lanterns,' said Ann.

As the flickering, yellow light penetrated the murk, casting vast, dismal shadows on the walls, Bird's Eye saw crates. 'That's where they must sleep,' he said. 'Suckers.'

Bradshaw nodded, and slung his crossbow over his back by a leather loop. He lifted the lid off one of the crates. 'Just as I thought,' he said. 'Nothing. They've all risen.'

'The moon is up outside,' said Bird's Eye. The words weren't out of his mouth before three Vampyrs rose out of the darkness, spitting and snarling. Candlelight cast sinister patterns on the ceiling and walls as the demons sprang from their hiding places, hissing and slashing with their talons.

'Shoot,' ordered Ann, giving the lead. 'Make every bolt count.'

Three quarrels, three kills.

'Don't drop your guard,' she warned. 'It isn't over.'

She was right. Through the half-light came half a dozen more, their red eyes blazing. The onrush of the ghouls claimed another victim.

'No!'

A man by the name of Beck was down, blood gurgling in his throat. Three of the creatures were around him, fangs bared. Bradshaw dispatched one while Bird's Eye took the second. But before Ann could finish the third, Beck was dead.

'They're still coming!'

Suddenly the bows were useless. The lightning-quick suckers were among them, flashing their deadly talons. Thinking quickly, Bradshaw snatched the sledgehammer he had used to smash down the outside door from one of the killing party. 'Everybody behind me,' he bawled. 'Ready with those bows.'

Sweat was glistening on his face and forearms. 'Blasted hell-fiends!' he roared. 'Back.' The swinging sledgehammer drove the Vampyrs back against the wall, where they crouched hissing. 'Bows!' The quarrels sang and the demons fell shrieking and flailing. Then the warehouse was silent, the only sound coming from water gushing from a broken gutter.

'Sweet heaven,' said Ann. 'How many more?'

There was no reply from Bird's Eye, only a hissing coming out of the murk.

'Lanterns,' cried Ann. 'Shine them over here.'

Bradshaw was raising the sledgehammer to break down a door when it burst inwards, flattening him with its weight. Two suckers were at him, their talons slicing through the sleeves of his jacket. They were leaning forward, lurching at him like polecats trying to flush a rabbit out of its warren.

'Get them off me!' It was a command, harsh and angry. Bradshaw wasn't a man who showed fear. Terror seemed to drive him into a savage fury.

The bolts crunched into the Vampyrs' decaying flesh, saving Bradshaw from their fangs, but the battle was still in the balance. The remaining suckers were spilling through the doorway at speed.

'Shoot!' screamed Ann, as a hideous ghoul-face loomed in front of her.

The battle raged on, but at the end of it all the Vampyrs lay dead. A few of the hunters were dabbing gingerly at slash-marks.

'Stake them all,' ordered Bradshaw, producing a flask of whisky. 'I don't want any nasty surprises.'

To the sound of points crunching into bone and flesh, Bradshaw poured alcohol over his mens' wounds. 'Ah, stop your squealing,' he snapped as they cried out in pain. 'It'll stop infection.' He took a swig of the burning liquid and looked around. 'We did it,' he observed. 'In spite of everything.'

Bird's Eye hung his head. He was waiting for Phoenix to add to his shame. But Phoenix had other things on his mind. 'Adams. Where's Adams?'

Bradshaw frowned.

'The Vampyr leader, the broodmaster. His body isn't here.' His words set off a frantic search. The Vampyr-hunters examined every crate, every recess.

'Anything?' asked Bradshaw. He got only shaken heads in reply. 'He's gone, Phoenix.'

Strangely, Phoenix seemed to have lost interest. He was looking at a printed sheet, stapled to one of the crates. It was a bill of lading.

'Where's Constanta?' he asked.

'Constanta,' said Ann. 'Let me see. It's a Black Sea port. That's where my father disembarked on his fatal journey to Csespa.' She folded the bill. 'We'll show this to Foxton.'

8

Back at the Foxton house, there was no sense of euphoria. Two men were dead, another badly injured. Then there was the question of Bird's Eye. But the casualties didn't blunt the group's determination. Rather, there was a renewed sense of purpose. Nobody doubted that they had won an important battle.

'Constanta,' said Foxton, inspecting the bill of lading. 'That's where Van Helsing and I began our ill-fated mission. The Legion is being recalled to Transylvania.' He was thinking of a mist-wreathed castle in the Carpathian foothills. The lair of Dracul. 'He expects us to follow.'

'Then we mustn't disappoint him,' said Phoenix.

'My dear boy,' said Foxton indulgently. 'You can't imagine what we will face there.'

'So tell me.'

Bradshaw and Laura were listening intently, as were the other Vampyr-hunters. Ann was comforting a distraught Bird's Eye in a corner of the room.

'When I close my eyes,' Foxton began, 'I can still see Csespa Castle. That is where Dracul is waiting. I see it as if it is right here in front of me, a monstrous building perched high on top of a rocky outcrop. It is surrounded by spruce and fir trees. The only approach to the castle is a rough track that winds up the steep hill. The walls are set with fortified gatehouses and there are towers at regular intervals all round the circumference. It is quite unlike a castle in our own country, however. The red-roofed buildings that rise from within the grey stone walls are of various designs. Three of them conical. The fourth is in the shape of a bell-tower.' He mopped at his brow with his handkerchief. The very mention of the word Csespa cast a shadow across his heart.

'There is a lime-washed barbican and there are slits here and there all around the fortifications, once used by crossbowmen to fire down at their enemies. Also set into the walls are small leaded windows, dust-grimed and dark like unblinking eyes. The entire building is alive with evil. It watches your approach, then devours you.'

Foxton placed his palms together, as if in prayer and rested his chin on his fingertips. 'That's Csespa.'

'It's decided then,' said Bradshaw. 'We pursue Dracul to his lair.'

Foxton looked into the coal fire and nodded. 'You're right. I only wish there were another way. I lost my greatest friend in that terrible place, the use of my legs too. We fought our way into Csespa, you see, all those years ago. In the depths of the castle we came across and slew a master Vampyr. The battle was long and hard. By the end, we believed we had destroyed Dracul himself. We were elated. We had cleansed the world of a dreadful plague. But just before dawn, as we camped in front of the castle, they came out of the heart of the night. Suckers by the score, rippers too. We lost a dozen men. We hadn't even posted a watch. What was the point? We had destroyed the head. The body would surely wither and die.'

He looked around. 'I had to witness Dracul killing Van Helsing. The creature laughed in my face and taunted me as he slashed my friend's throat.'

Ann looked away.

'Then he came for me. His strength was superhuman. He picked me up like a rag doll and hurled me from the walls of Csespa. He left me for dead on the rocks below.'

'Then we must return for two reasons,' said Bradshaw, 'To destroy this plague and to avenge Van Helsing. This time there will be no mistake. We will destroy him and all his kind.'

Foxton nodded. 'You're right of course. We must return.'

'But are we capable of such a mission?' asked Ann. 'After all, it was only yesterday that we were staring defeat in the face. Now we are preparing a crusade into the Carpathian mountains.'

'I've told you,' said Phoenix impatiently, supporting Bradshaw. 'There is no choice. If we fail . . .'

'Yes,' said Ann. 'I understand the consequences.'

'This project *is* achievable,' said Foxton, interrupting them. 'But it will require the coordination of all our resources. Our frail forces would suffer total annihilation by themselves. The Committee of Nine must be reformed. We will provide the heart of the organization.'

'We?'

'Myself, Ann, of course, and Bradshaw.'

Bradshaw gave Foxton a sideways glance.

'You Phoenix will be number four. Our European contacts will take up the five remaining places.'

'How soon can this be done?' asked Phoenix.

'I will send off the telegrams today,' said Foxton. 'Five of the Committee will be instructed to meet us in Marseille within the month. The remaining, and most important member will meet us at Constanta.'

'And who is he?' asked Bradshaw. 'Who is this final member?'

'His name is Nikolai Dimitrescu,' said Foxton. 'He was our guide to Csespa on that last ill-fated journey. He was also the most cautious and far-sighted of us. We couldn't convince him that the master we had slain was truly Dracul. Had he not left us to search the grounds of the castle for surviving Vampyrs, he might have suffered Professor Van Helsing's fate. He discovered me in the gorge below the castle.'

Foxton ran his fingers through his hair. 'I owe him my life.'

'And he can be trusted?'

'He has fought the Vampyr all his adult life,' said Foxton,

dismissing Phoenix's caution. 'He and his troupe of Szekely horse have resisted the demon plague right at its very heart.'

'It is decided then,' said Phoenix, rising to his feet. 'That leaves us with one piece of unfinished business.' He picked up a knife from the table and advanced on Bird's Eye.

'Phoenix, no!' He found his way blocked by Laura and Bradshaw.

'This isn't the way,' said Bradshaw.

Phoenix stared in bewilderment at their reaction. 'You don't think . . . ?'

He threw his head back and laughed. 'I'm not intending to hurt him. Quite the opposite, I want to save him.' He was met by questioning looks. 'He bears a mark,' Phoenix explained. 'Like the one on Mrs Cave. That's how the Gamesmaster controls minds and plants his own ideas. I have seen it before, in another world. The only thing to do is cut it out.'

'Cut it out?' cried Ann, horrified.

'Either that or the Gamesmaster continues to twist Robert's thoughts. May I?' Bird's Eye submitted to Phoenix's examination. 'Here.' He lifted Bird's Eye's fine blond hair to reveal a tattoo-like mark, no bigger than a finger-nail. It was in the shape of a bat.

'But how?' cried Ann. 'I have never seen this blemish. I would have noticed.'

'Have you been sick recently, or woken up feeling different?' Phoenix asked Bird's Eye.

'Yes,' said Bird's Eye. 'Two months ago. I was down with a fever for several days. It was while I was away at boarding school.'

'Then there was the opportunity,' said Phoenix. He held up the knife. 'Shall I continue?'

'Do what you have to,' said Bird's Eye. 'I won't be used by the fiend another day.'

Later that evening, while the fire was burning low, Bird's Eye dozed, a dressing applied to the back of his neck. Ann was watching over him. Phoenix was about to go up to bed when he noticed Laura slip away. Leaving Foxton and Bradshaw poring over a map of central Europe, he followed her to a large window at the end of the landing.

'Something wrong?'

'It's what Foxton said,' Laura told him. 'We'll be in Marseille within the month. The *month*, Phoenix.'

'You're thinking about home?'

'Of course.'

'I know it probably won't help much,' said Phoenix, 'But if it's like our last adventure, time hasn't changed there. Everything that happens here, whether it is weeks or months, it all goes by in the blink of an eye in our world. Your parents don't even know you've gone.'

Laura nodded. 'I understand that.'

'It doesn't help, does it?' said Phoenix sympathetically.

Laura turned and shook her head. There were tears in her eyes.

A universe away, in a nondescript market town called Brownleigh, John and Christina Graves were living in that blink of an eye, watching their son's progress through a dangerous and frightening world. The time on every clock in the house registered the same moment as when Phoenix had vanished into the computer. The traffic, the trees, the birds in the sky were all caught in freeze-frame. They felt no desire to eat or drink. There was no need to leave the computer screen. Though they could move and watch and talk, they, as much as anything else in the house, were subject to the suspension of time. And as they watched, the picture on the screen faded, crowded out by a snowstorm of threes, sixes and nines.

It was a message.

So it is on to Level Two, the realm of the undead. My domain. Keep coming, young Legendeer, hurry on into my dark embrace. How eagerly you race towards me. Towards your death.

97

BOOK THREE

The Book of the Undead

1

The new Committee that met a month later in Constanta numbered eight. Dim candlelight lit their unsmiling faces as the brief dusk came and went. The rest of the party, including Laura and Bird's Eye, sat listening from the shadows.

'So where is he?' Phoenix asked rising from his chair and paced the floor. 'Where is Dimitrescu?'

'He will be here,' said Foxton. He waved his hands, palms down, but the calming gesture had precisely the opposite effect.

'Well, I don't like it,' Phoenix snapped. He felt the weight of their undertaking like an unbearable burden. 'This is important. Doesn't he know what's at stake here? He could at least be on time.'

The weeks of waiting had taken its toll on Phoenix. He was at his best when he was able to give himself up to instinct, to fight at the bidding of his ancestry. In those moments, when he responded compulsively, nothing could stop him. It was when he had time to dwell on the enormity of the task ahead that the modern teenager surfaced, sapping his will. Then he would fret and come close to despair. The train journeys, evenings spent kicking his heels in hotel rooms, the endless days at sea had driven him to distraction.

'Well, I say we get started without him,' said Bradshaw who, for all his fifty years, was also champing at the bit.

'No,' said the Swede Andersen. 'The quorum of this Committee is nine. All members must be present before such a crusade is launched. I say we wait.' His words won a murmur of approval. Phoenix, who had barely been persuaded back to his seat, leapt up and stamped to the window. He looked out, taking in the strange sights and smells of the small port. Night had fallen, and here and there in the inky blackness fires flared and candles glowed. What light showed under the central European sky seemed almost apologetic, dwarfed by the endless power of the dark.

'Wait!' Phoenix snarled. 'That's all we ever do. And while we wait, our enemy is gathering his forces. We have to strike, Foxton, and soon.'

'Oh, we will strike,' said Foxton, composed and patient as ever. 'But without Dimitrescu we would be going blind into Dracul's domain. I am not willing to throw this expedition to the wolves.'

Some of the Committee were exchanging anxious glances. They hadn't expected discord so early in the mission. In addition to Phoenix, Foxton, Bradshaw and Ann Van Helsing, seated around the table were Andersen, Schreck from Germany, a Bulgarian by the name of Sakarov and a squat Hungarian, Tibor Puskas. It was Puskas who spoke next. He stood formally, adjusting his waistcoat.

'Gentlemen, and ladies. We are all united in our aims. We have come from every corner of Europe to destroy the demonlord. Let us have no arguments please. Discord can only blunt our purpose.'

Phoenix scowled.

You're out there somewhere. Dracul.

You, Adams.

And you. Gamesmaster. A trinity of evil.

'Please resume your seat, Phoenix,' said Foxton. 'If Dimitrescu is late, then he has good reason.' The way he said it hinted at some undeclared item of business, something between Foxton and Dimitrescu alone.

'Really?'

'Yes Phoenix,' said Foxton, 'really. There isn't a day that Dimitrescu hasn't faced the Vampyr, or at least felt its shadow fall across his life. He is a Transylvanian. He grew up with the icy breath of the demon on the back of his neck. He will be here.'

Phoenix was about to reply when he heard hoofbeats on the cobbled streets. Half a dozen horsemen were galloping wildly down the streets, as if pursued by all the fiends of Hell, sending passers-by scurrying for safety.

'Now that,' said Foxton with a broad smile, 'sounds like Nikolai. He does like to stage a dramatic entrance. There are those who say he can trace his ancestors back to the Mongol hordes of Genghis Khan.'

Phoenix watched the riders dismount. Three of them immediately took up positions at the front door of the tavern. Two more jogged round the back. His impatience and suspicion began to melt away. The speed and efficiency with which the horsemen inspected and then sealed the exits from the building reassured him. The group's sense of purpose and energy was almost tangible. Giving the street one last look, the sixth man marched into the tavern. He entered without knocking.

He wasn't tall, and his peasant's clothes were rough and ill-fitting. He was quite dark-skinned and had a thick moustache. His cheekbones were high and his features almost Asiatic. Set down on paper, none of this makes him particularly noteworthy, but the reality of the Vampyr-hunger was different. The sum of all those parts, when brought together, added up to one of the most striking men Phoenix had ever seen.

'I,' said the man standing in the doorway, 'am Nikolai Dimitrescu.'

An hour later, agreement had all but been reached.

'Though the roads are not good,' Dimitrescu argued, 'I am convinced that you should come with us, Ramsay. You will be able to complete the journey by carriage. If you were to stay behind in Constanta, you would be vulnerable to the Vampyr's

103

attacks. We will all be exposed out there, but at least there is strength in numbers.'

Foxton laughed. 'I did so hope you would say that, Nikolai. I have spent too many years holed up in my study. It is time I was in action once more. After all, you don't need legs to shoot a crossbow.'

Phoenix was feeling better. Dimitrescu was decisive and committed to an attack on Csespa. 'What about Csespa?' Phoenix asked. 'If Dracul is there, why did you miss him last time?'

'The castle is huge,' Dimitrescu replied, stung by the criticism, especially when it came from a teenage boy. 'It is honeycombed with hundreds of passages and rooms. There are false walls and secret entrances. The entire place is a vast labyrinth.'

Phoenix and Laura exchanged glances. They knew all about labyrinths!

'But the creature we encountered was a murderous opponent. His minions defended him fang and talon, as if he truly were the Father of Darkness. The struggle was long and hard, and many a good man fell. The stubbornness of their resistance convinced us we had slain Dracul. Had you been there, you would have forgiven us our mistake.'

Phoenix nodded. 'I believe you. The one we seek is a master of illusion.'

Dimitrescu looked at Phoenix, as if appraising him, then ran his gaze over the members of the Committee. 'Like the darkness in which the monster lives,' he said, 'Dracul plays tricks on the eye and on the mind.'

'Did you ever return to Csespa?' asked Phoenix. 'Have you ever been back?'

Dimitrescu shook his head. 'To the castle, no, but I recently rode through the district. The darkness is strong there. There are many *moroi*.'

'*Moroi*?' asked Phoenix.

'Yes,' said Dimitrescu, '*moroi*.'

'The *moroi* are the undead,' Foxton explained. 'It is a far more common term in these parts than Vampyr.'

'Only a brave man travels the roads of Csespa in the hours of daylight,' said Dimitrescu. 'And after dark, none at all. The villagers shutter their windows and bolt their doors. There is precious little hospitality in that region.'

'So what you're saying is . . .'

'What I am saying,' Dimitrescu said, 'is that tomorrow we shall be riding into the jaws of Hell.'

2

The Vampyr-hunters left Constanta at the crack of dawn, hoping to slip out of the port unnoticed. By the time they set off, however, scattering the nightbirds by their progress, a substantial crowd had gathered to watch their departure. The four score spectators who had gathered at the tavern watched in silence, but you could almost touch their expectation. The front of the column was made up of Dimitrescu's Szekely cavalry, unsmiling men in grimy jackets and fur caps. The bodyguards who had accompanied Dimitrescu the night before had been supplemented by twenty more. They had spent the night at an inn on the edge of town. One of them was holding the reins of a cart, tightly bound tarpaulins hiding its cargo. Next came the Committee and Bird's Eye. They too were on horseback. Finally, clattering along with outriders to front and rear, was the carriage bearing Ramsay Foxton. Phoenix and Laura had joined Foxton inside, hitching their mounts to the coach. At the final crossroads on the edge of the town, an old man stepped forward, seemingly oblivious to the oncoming horses.

'Is it true what they say?' he asked, planting himself in their way. 'You go to slay the *moroi*?'

'What business is it of yours?' demanded Dimitrescu, reining back his steed.

'Only this,' the old man replied. 'I have just arrived from my home in Csespa. I was driven out by the *moroi*. The undead killed my wife and daughter. There is only one thing I want from my life, and that is to see this land cleansed of the *moroi*.

Take this token. It will convince the people of Csespa that you are serious in your undertaking.' He produced a wooden figurine. It represented a young girl, sleeping with her arms crossed over her breast. The foot of the statuette had been carved into a deadly point, like a stake. 'It is from the wood of the fir tree. You understand its significance, your honour?'

For a moment, the old man stared at Dimitrescu as if he recognized him. Then Dimitrescu nodded and accepted the offering before waving the column on. Phoenix and Foxton looked back, watching the old man disappear into the mist of daybreak.

'Why a fir tree?' Laura asked out loud.

Turning away from the window, Foxton answered her: 'There is a custom in Transylvania of planting a fir tree above a Vampyr's grave. The root is meant to pierce the heart of the undead buried beneath.'

Laura shuddered. 'I wish I hadn't asked.'

'No, my dear, don't try to shut it out. If you are to survive in these parts, you must face the truth, however ugly.'

'Fine,' said Laura. 'So you want me to scare myself silly. Tell me about Csespa then. What are we getting ourselves into?'

'The village lies in a bleak corner of the Carpathian foothills. It abounds with tales of the undead. There are three manifestations of the ghoul.'

Three.

'The *moroi*, the male, you have already heard about,' Foxton continued, unaware of the significance of the number. 'The feminine form of the demon is the *strigoi*. Then there is a creature which changes into animal form, such as a dog or a wolf, the *pricolici*.'

'The Wolver,' said Laura.

Phoenix was preoccupied, still reflecting on the way the three forms of the Vampyr mirrored the number patterns that ran through the myth-world.

'Quite,' said Foxton, smiling at Laura. 'The Wolver. We will find the moon-born waiting like a hellish watchdog, guarding the approaches to Csespa. Towering over the village is the castle itself. It is much more like a stone pile. It is a silent, brooding reminder of the Vampyr's presence. Though the local people hate the ghoulish plague that has blighted their lives for generations they do not take kindly to strangers and refused point blank to cooperate with our last expedition.'

'So we will be on our own?'

'Unfortunately, yes.'

Some hours later they took a winding path through an entangled forest. In the woodland gloom, conversation died. It was only after they had been moving through the woods for over half an hour that Laura spoke.

'How far is it to Csespa?'

'Two days' ride,' said Foxton, 'Given favourable conditions. We will rest overnight at Buzau, then go on into Transylvania tomorrow.'

'The last time you made this journey,' Phoenix asked, 'how long before the demons started taking notice of you?'

'Oh, they've been watching us ever since we disembarked,' said Foxton. 'You can be certain of that. But if you are asking about the attacks, they began the second night, a few hours ride from Csespa.'

'But you fought them off?'

'Yes, we won our skirmishes, both on our way to the castle and within. Looking back, however, I can't help but wonder whether the whole thing wasn't all an elaborate charade, a trick to put us off the scent of Dracul himself.'

'So you expect it to be harder this time?' asked Laura.

'Yes, my dear,' said Foxton candidly. 'I expect our approach to bring a tempest down around our heads. Darkness will strike back with all the fury it has at its disposal. But we have two advantages. First, our young friend, Bird's Eye. We will have need of that sixth sense of his.'

'So you believe Bird's Eye is free of the Gamesmaster's control?' Laura asked.

'Yes, I am quite sure he is.'

'You mentioned *two* advantages,' said Phoenix.

'That's right,' said Foxton, his eyes twinkling. 'The other is your good self.'

'Me!'

'Of course. That is why I still believe young Robert's vision. No false modesty, please. You have added an extra dimension to our cause. At last we have an explanation for the Vampyr's actions. We believed him to be engaged in wanton destructivness and evil. Now we can see more clearly. He has a purpose, the invasion of your world, and that means he has a weakness too. In your own way, you have insights every bit as important as Robert's. Ann and Bradshaw have both remarked on it. You meet the Vampyr's ruthlessness with a determination every bit as pitiless. You anticipate his actions. You were born for this.'

There it was again, the rumour of destiny. Phoenix looked away and stared out through the screen of fir trees towards the distant mountains.

Is that what I am to become, a pitiless hunter?

He watched the sun's progress behind the tall trunks. It was a pale yellow orb, following them. It reminded him of an eye, an unblinking, all-seeing eye. Like the eye of the Gamesmaster.

'Foxton,' he asked, without turning. 'How do you rate our chances?'

Foxton smiled grimly. 'Better than ten to one, worse than evens. Does that answer your question?'

Phoenix felt a tremor go through him.

There is no going back. Your destiny awaits you.

He met Foxton's eyes. 'It isn't the answer I would have liked, but it's an honest one. When the time comes, I will be ready.'

Foxton smiled. 'I never doubted it for a moment.'

3

The innkeeper accepted their custom without question. Not so his patrons. The moment they laid eyes on the Szekelys, they started to point and shift uneasily in their seats. Dimitrescu said something to them in gruff Romanian.

'What was all that about?' asked Laura.

'The words are too coarse for a young lady's ears,' Puskas told her. '*Good night, gentlemen,* would be an adequate translation.'

Ann shook her head while the German Shreck chuckled mischievously.

'How many nights will your honour and his entourage be staying?' asked the innkeeper, trying in vain to disguise his unease.

'Just the one,' said Foxton, taking over from Dimitrescu. He seemed keen not to ruffle the locals' feathers. His bridge-building didn't get very far. It was immediately undone when Dimitrescu set down the figurine given him that morning on the road out of Constanta. The handful of men who had been drinking at the tables got up noisily and left. The innkeeper shrank back, crossing himself.

'You seek the *moroi*?' he gasped.

'That's right,' said Ann. 'We do.'

'Then you must go,' the innkeeper said in a barely audible whisper. 'You will bring the night-plague down on this house.'

Foxton was about to negotiate, but Dimitrescu made his intentions clear by planting himself at a table and putting his feet up.

'I think that means we're staying,' Bradshaw announced, taking a seat opposite Dimitrescu.

'Stay then,' said the innkeeper. 'But you will be alone. After dark, they will come. And, believe me, when they do no sane man would choose to be here. My wife and I will leave you now. Anything you find in my humble inn, you may have. You have the run of the place. It is the privilege of dead souls.'

The speech cut little ice with Ann, Foxton, Bradshaw and the Szekelys, but Bird's Eye and Laura listened wide-eyed.

'We will stay with family until you are gone. I would be grateful if you would pay your board in advance.' He took his money. 'Thank you. And may God have mercy on your soul.' Whipping off his apron, he started barking orders to his wife and staff. Within minutes, the place was virtually empty.

'You will rue the day you passed this way,' hissed the innkeeper, in his broken English. 'I warned the Darkman, but he wouldn't listen. He never returned.'

Dimitrescu and Bradshaw laughed, but Phoenix didn't. He stared after the innkeeper as he hurried away.

'Something wrong?' asked Foxton.

The Darkman. Or a man called Darke?

Phoenix was after him in a split second. 'Wait,' he cried. 'Tell me about the Darkman. I want to know about him.'

'I have nothing to say to you.'

Phoenix drew the Angel of Death. 'Oh, I think you do. Now, the Darkman.'

The innkeeper sighed. 'He was like you, a stranger. English. He came alone. If you are interested he left some of his belongings in his room. They are behind the counter.' He stretched out a hand. 'A few coins and they are yours.'

Phoenix scowled, and offered him nothing. 'I want to know about the Darkman.'

'We warned him of the dangers, but he just laughed. He treated the *moroi* as a joke. It was all a game to him.'

That's right. A game. And it killed him.

111

'When the Darkman left, he wasn't alone. He was being followed.'

'Followed? Who by?'

'A *moroi* such as I have never seen. One who walks by day.'

Phoenix started.

Adams.

'I wanted to warn the Darkman,' the innkeeper babbled. 'But I feared the consequences. You must understand, I have a family.'

Phoenix waved him on his way with the stock of the Angel. 'Yes, I understand.'

'What was all that about?' asked Foxton, the moment Phoenix walked back in.

'We're not the only ones to come in search of Csespa castle,' said Phoenix. He glanced at Laura. 'A man from our world, Chris Darke, came this way recently.' Laura gasped. Meanwhile, Phoenix stepped behind the counter and pulled out the innkeeper's ledger. 'Yes, here's his name.'

Foxton looked at the signature, then flicked the page back and forward. 'You mean he came alone?'

'That's right.'

'One man?'

'One man.'

'Was he mad?'

'No,' said Laura, 'Not mad. But he didn't have a clue what he was letting himself in for.'

Foxton frowned.

'The computer we told you about,' Phoenix explained. 'The machine that brought us here. This piece of equipment . . .' He showed them the points bracelet. 'He uses them to turn the events here into a game.'

'A game!' roared Bradshaw indignantly. 'A game, you say? Odd sort of game that has murdered so many of my comrades.'

'I promise you,' said Phoenix, 'That's it, a complex, addictive and deadly game. That's how the Gamesmaster is going to open the gateway between the worlds . . .'

'By disguising it as an entertainment?' asked Bradshaw incredulously.

'That's right.'

Phoenix searched for Chris Darke's belongings. He laid them out and gave a low whistle.

'What is it?'

'His notebook. See these numbers?' he indicated a row of threes, sixes and nines.

'This is the language of the game.'

'Ah,' said Foxton. '*Omnia in numeris sita sunt.*'

'I beg your pardon?'

'A phrase from the ancient science of numerology: everything lies veiled in numbers. They say . . .'

Foxton's explanation was cut short. Bird's Eye suddenly stumbled against the counter. 'I see it,' he said. 'I see the gateway between the worlds. It came when you mentioned the numbers.'

'You see it? How?'

'For a moment, I glimpsed how it opens. I saw both you and Laura standing before it. Don't believe me? Then I'll describe it to you. I see a golden portal, multiples of three etched in silvery light around the edge of the gateway. Is that it?'

'Yes,' Phoenix replied. 'That's it exactly. But where?'

'Give me a moment,' said Bird's Eye. 'Yes, I see a room with an exit but no entrance. That's where the gate can be opened.'

'An exit but no entrance,' Laura repeated. 'Now he's started talking in riddles. What's that supposed to mean?'

Bird's Eye shook his head. 'I don't know, but it's up there . . .'

He looked out of the window at the evening mist stealing like smoke up the mountainside. 'It's in Csespa castle!'

4

The Legion came an hour before dawn. Bird's Eye had predicted as much about ninety minutes earlier, starting from his troubled sleep with a cry of terror. The mind-pictures tore through him. He didn't understand at the time why his announcement hadn't generated more excitement. There was a burst of activity around the doors and windows as eyes searched for an invisible enemy, but as the minutes ticked away, most people soon slipped back into an exhausted sleep. Only Phoenix, Bradshaw and the Szekelys remained alert at their posts. When the attack finally came, it was the Wolvers first, smashing their way through the wooden shutters of the tavern as if bursting through a paper screen. Such was the speed of the assault, that Bird's Eye had barely had time to shout a warning before they were inside the building.

'Rippers!'

They roared ferociously, unleashing a din that thundered in his skull until he staggered back from the pain of it. His throat was so dry and tight, he could imagine what it would be like to be strangled from within. He had predicted this. So why had they done so little? Why weren't they better prepared?

'Help me!'

Bird's Eye had edged towards the windows just before the attack. Unwisely, he had neglected to take his crossbow with him.

'Help!'

The nearest of the beasts exploded into the air, snapping and snorting with all the blind savagery of a hurricane. It was upon

Bird's Eye in an instant, pinning him to the floor with a huge paw. The needle points of its fangs began to close over him.

'No!'

Phoenix was coming at the run, bringing down the ripper with a single shot from the Angel. Bird's Eye gratefully scrambled from under its terrible weight. By the time he got to his feet the room was a confusion of clattering bolts, waving torches and snapping Wolvers. The first skirmish barely lasted two minutes and ended with every one of the rippers lying dead.

Ann turned towards her son. 'Is it over?'

Bird's Eye shook his head. 'It has barely even begun. Take a look if you wish. Out there.'

Laura ran to the nearest window. 'Oh no!' she cried.

There in the moonlight were more Wolvers. Twenty of them. Battle-strength. Their baying echoing and re-echoing round the walls of the town square. The Vampyr were following, their eerie, almost featureless faces gleaming in the half-light. Bird's Eye tried to control his galloping heart. He picked up his bow and clutched it hard.

'What happened to Dimitrescu and his men?' he demanded. 'They were all here an hour ago and now they're nowhere to be seen. And where's Bradshaw?'

This time he wasn't sure what he was seeing. There was something, definitely something. A shifting in the darkness. Grey etched against black. But whether it was friend or foe, he just couldn't say.

'Why don't they attack?' asked Laura, staring at the ranks of the demons. Her face was gleaming with a sheen of sweat.

Phoenix smiled and walked behind the counter. 'They're looking for the Szekelys.'

While Laura was still wondering what there was to smile about, Phoenix laid the Angel on the floor and took a longbow from its hiding place behind the counter. 'Now, Bradshaw,' he shouted.

Bradshaw appeared from a side room. He lit the end of the

115

specially prepared arrow and handed it over. Drawing the bowstring to his ear, Phoenix moved to the window and shot high into the air, tracing an arc of light over the square.

'What are you doing?' demanded Laura.

The rippers and suckers were pushing and jostling, staring at the arrow's fiery path.

'What's going on?'

Phoenix tapped his nose. 'You'll see.'

Which is exactly what Bird's Eye did at that very moment. He saw.

He saw Dimitrescu and his men emerging from doorways all around the square. He saw the flaming arrows being aimed and fired at the encircled ghouls. He saw a fiery ring of death. 'You knew about this!' he cried.

Phoenix nodded. 'Of course I did.'

'You knew?' Laura repeated. 'You knew, and you didn't say anything!'

Phoenix walked straight past his friends. 'What was there to say? You were dozing off again. We had to make preparations.'

'You could have kept us awake,' Laura retorted. 'We had a right to know what you were doing.'

'I haven't got time to stand here arguing the toss,' said Phoenix. 'A few of us decided to act on the information Bird's Eye gave us. It allowed you to snatch some sleep. Now, we can argue the rights and wrongs of our decision later, if you want. But we've got a fight on our hands. The battle isn't over yet.'

It was true. The monsters in the middle of the square had been destroyed but more were massing in the side streets, hissing and baying, tensing for the final charge. It was beyond the Vampyr-hunters' worst imaginings.

'So many,' murmured Bird's Eye.

Like an ocean of death.

Vampyr fliers were settling on the rooftops, ready to plunge down and feed on the people below. Laura, Bird's Eye and Ann exchanged glances and followed Phoenix outside. Dimitrescu and his men had saddled up and were forming a line, blazing arrows aimed at the advancing monsters. The rest of the Vampyr-hunters took up positions along the wall of the inn, bows trained on the Legion's ranks.

Then it began, the hammer-blow onslaught of the Wolvers and the shrieking, hissing attacks of the Vampyrs. The Szekelys thinned the demon ranks with their death-torches, but their arrows could not halt the Legion's advance. Puskas fell first, screaming hideously as he was carried off by a Wolver. Schreck was taken moments later, caught unawares when a Vampyr burst from a darkened doorway. Within seconds he was overwhelmed by a pack of suckers.

'There are too many!' screamed Andersen.

He was right. The advantage the Vampyr-hunters had won by surprise was being lost because of the overwhelming superiority of the Legion's numbers.

'Get inside!' yelled Dimitrescu, motioning to his men to dismount.

The second phase of the battle had begun. The Szekelys defended the ground floor, everyone else the first floor. The Wolvers were propelling themselves forward in furious waves, crashing into the walls, and though the defenders' bolts and arrows took a heavy toll, the momentum of the attack never slowed. The Vampyrs added their own contribution, spitting and screeching as they swarmed over the roof and upper balconies, trying to gain entry.

'Ann, Bird's Eye, Laura,' yelled Phoenix, running downstairs from the upper floor, 'come with me.'

'You need us now then?' Laura retorted, not yet ready to forget the way he had left her in the dark.

'Are you coming or not?'

Bird's Eye almost dropped his bow as he reached the top of the stairs. In the thirty seconds it had taken Phoenix to summon them, the suckers had broken through, driving Sakarov and Andersen from their positions and onto the landing.

'Get back!' yelled Phoenix.

The men flattened themselves against the wall and the crossbow bolts hissed their lethal message.

'Where's Bradshaw?' shouted Phoenix as he reloaded. 'And Foxton?'

'In here,' shouted Foxton. 'Quick!'

Phoenix and Bird's Eye almost collided with Bradshaw as he backed towards the door. He was engaged in hand-to-hand fighting with two Vampyrs. As Sakarov followed Phoenix into the room, Ann cried out in terror. Over their shoulders she had seen Foxton being dragged towards the window.

'Stop them!'

Phoenix raised the Angel, but his shot was blocked by Bradshaw as he wrestled off one of his assailants and dispatched it with a stake. Ann pushed past the pair of them and shot the Vampyr to Foxton's left. It gave him the chance to get a handhold on the window frame. Bird's Eye and Laura took the remaining ghouls and Foxton fell heavily to the ground.

'Thank you,' he panted, grimacing with pain.

But still the battle raged as more and more suckers swarmed through the windows and down through holes they had torn in the roof.

'We're not holding them!' shrieked Andersen as three suckers surrounded him. 'It's finished.' But nobody else believed they were finished.

Bradshaw was fighting like a madman, with stake and hatchet. Sakarov joined him, and the two stood back to back, taking on the Vampyrs in close combat, while Ann, Bird's Eye and Laura did their best to keep out further Vampyrs with steady volleys of crossbow quarrels. Satisfied that they were holding their own, Phoenix ran to Andersen.

'Get off him!'

The suckers were clinging to him, ripping and tearing at one another in their feeding frenzy. Phoenix shot his bolt into the nearest of them, then hammered a stake into the second. The third came up at him, spitting and snarling. The sheer power of the attack caught him off balance and the boy and fiend tumbled fighting down the stairs. As they hit the floor at the bottom, Phoenix saw the creature above him. Its eyes were like dark stones, its fangs curved and dripping venom.

'No!'

As the Vampyr lunged forward, he smelt the sour death-decay on its breath.

'No!'

Then it shuddered. It threw back its head and shrieked. A flaming arrow was sticking out of its back. It was the work of Dimitrescu. Suddenly the roaring and shrieking was abating, replaced by a strange rustling and crackling.

'What's happening?' Phoenix asked.

'They're retreating,' said Dimitrescu, wiping the sweat from his forehead. 'It's dawn.'

5

By the time the townspeople finally decided it was safe to emerge from their homes, the funeral pyres of Schreck and Puskas were burning fiercely in the town square, sending a plume of grey smoke into the clear morning sky. Bradshaw, always businesslike, had begun the process of purification within minutes of the Legion's forced retreat. The innkeeper was among the first to approach the Vampyr-hunters, eyes bulging and arms windmilling in a show of outrage.

'See the destruction you have brought upon our town,' he cried. 'Look what you've done to my tavern.'

Foxton shook his head wearily and threw something to Dimitrescu to pass on.

'Here,' said Dimitrescu, depositing a fat purse in the innkeeper's hand. 'Now stop whining. There will be enough here to return your wretched tavern to normal. Take it and get on with your miserable, little life. You should be thanking us for what we have done, not ranting on about your precious building. Roofs and windows can easily be mended, but what about broken bodies and shattered lives? Nothing short of bitter struggle will drive the Vampyr from our land.'

'You can't end the horror,' shouted a priest who had been listening from the church doorway opposite. 'We have endured the *moroi* for centuries. Evil never sleeps, my friend. We will have to learn to live with it for many more. Go home. We don't want you here.'

'What?' cried Dimitrescu, 'Endurance, is that all you can offer? Is that the way you want your people to live? Will you really permit the endless slaughter of innocents? No, I will not go away. Our crusade will continue.'

The innkeeper seemed to speak for most of the townspeople. 'Well, we want none of it. All you are going to do is bring worse disaster down about our heads. So the blood-suckers take the odd unfortunate. The rest of us go on living, don't we? We bury our dead and struggle on. Now, clear out and leave us to repair the damage.'

Dimitrescu shook his head. As he passed Phoenix, he spoke sadly. 'Not all my people are such cowards.'

'They're not cowards,' Phoenix replied. 'Just too terrified to fight back. We have to show them the darkness can be defeated.'

Dimitrescu nodded grimly. 'That's just what I have been trying to do for twenty long years, and I'm growing tired.'

'There's a difference,' said Phoenix. 'This time we can finish it.'

'You really believe that?'

Phoenix remembered Bird's Eye's vision of the gateway and the glowing numbers. Csespa castle was only a day's ride away. It was up there amid the dense carpet of pine and spruce and the rolling mist, and it held the promise of a reckoning with the Gamesmaster and the journey home.

'Yes, this time we really can finish it.'

Dimitrescu shoved his way past the hostile townspeople and started inspecting the horses. Phoenix watched the Szekely leader patting his own horse and talking soothingly to it. Then, detaching himself from the complaining innkeeper, he sought out Laura.

'Still mad at me?'

'Not really,' she answered. 'I just felt you were treating me like a kid last night.'

'We didn't want to make too much of a song and dance,' Phoenix explained. 'We could have alerted the Legion to what we were doing. Then . . .' He paused. 'It doesn't bear thinking about.'

Laura turned to look at him. 'You're changing.'

'Am I?'

'You don't talk to me as much as you used to. You hardly act like a teenager any more. You were always serious. Now . . .'

'Yes,' said Phoenix, 'I know what you mean.'

My destiny. It's coming.

Laura spoke again: 'Adams didn't join the fight last night.'

'No,' said Phoenix. 'I've been wondering about that myself. He and Dracul will be at Csespa, at the Gamesmaster's side.'

The trinity of evil.

'So it's true what Ann just told me,' she said.

'What's that?'

'Last night was just the first round. There's worse to come.'

'No doubt about it,' said Phoenix, sensing the darkness coiled and restless beyond the mountain tops. 'The closer we come to Dracul's lair, the more ferociously he is going to defend it.'

Goaded by the none-too-friendly attentions of the towns-folk, Dimitrescu was hurrying along the preparations for the group's departure. Two of his men were lifting Foxton into his carriage. The old man was nursing cuts and bruises from the previous night's fighting. Others were securing the tarpaulins covering the cart's mysterious cargo.

'It looks like we're about to leave,' said Laura, walking towards the carriage. 'Coming?'

Phoenix shook his head. 'I'm going to ride today,' he said. 'I need to think.'

Laura smiled. 'OK.' She was about to climb into the carriage when she saw Andersen lifting himself into the stirrups. His movements were heavy and awkward. He seemed to have fared even worse than Foxton. 'What's the matter with him?'

'He came within an inch of being the third casualty last night,' said Phoenix. 'Three suckers had him pinned down. I killed two of them. Dimitrescu got the other.'

'Lucky man,' said Laura before joining Foxton in the carriage.

But if she had taken a closer look, Laura would have quickly changed her mind. As Andersen spurred his mount forward through the muttering crowds, he scratched at his neck. The irritation came from two raised blisters on his throat, just above the collar bone. They were a mixed black and crimson colour and they were seeping. The bruising around the puncture marks had taken on a familiar shape, that of a bat. Phoenix was wrong. Andersen hadn't come close to being the third casualty of the Vampyr attack.

He *was* the third casualty.

6

As the Vampyr hunters started their climb up the wooded slopes, the weather changed. Driving rain forced the riders to don capes and wide-brimmed hats and bend beneath the lashing storm.

'Welcome to Transylvania,' said Dimitrescu, gesturing towards the cheerless mountainside. The Szekelys didn't betray a flicker of emotion. It was different for the hunters. They blinked against the icy rain, as if trying to make out the shapes of the undead among the trees. They were entering the heart of darkness.

'See anything?' Laura asked Bird's Eye.

'Nothing,' he replied. 'Not the slightest hint of a vision. Maybe it's the fear.'

Yes, thought Phoenix, *maybe it is the fear*. He was feeling it too. It was all coming together.

His destiny.

His fear.

They passed through a hamlet. It was quite deserted, or so it seemed. Every house was shuttered and not a soul walked the dirt track that served as a main street. The hunters rode on, leaving its occupants cowering behind the shutters. As the miles passed, a feeling of gloom and foreboding crept into every heart. Phoenix was no exception. He felt it stealing through him like an icy dart. But he felt something else.

Expectation.

Up ahead, beyond the dark waves of trees, beyond the

glistening, silvery rain, his enemy was waiting. Slowly, imperceptibly Phoenix fell back from his comrades. He was content to bring up the rear, cast adrift among his own thoughts.

It was there, in the trembling darkness, a room with an exit but no entrance. It was a place made equally of horror and of hope; a trap and a gateway.

Soon we will meet.

Phoenix brushed the rain from his eyes and stared ahead. The rider in front of him had slowed and the two of them were becoming separated from the main column. He spurred his horse to a canter.

'Hey,' he said, coming up on the shoulder of the rider. 'We're falling behind.' He saw that it was Andersen, slumped low in the saddle, most of his face buried in his cape. 'Are you all right?' Andersen gave a moan and slid from his saddle, tumbling to the ground like a heavy bundle. 'What's the matter?' Phoenix asked anxiously. 'Are you ill?' He dismounted and rolled Andersen over. 'Andersen.' There was no reply. The Swede's breathing was slow and laboured. 'Andersen!' Phoenix stood up and shouted after the column, but they were already out of earshot. 'Listen Andersen,' he said, bending down to speak directly into the man's ear. 'You've got to give me a hand.'

But Andersen was in no shape to give anyone a hand. Phoenix looked at his pale, waxy skin and found himself in an agony of indecision. He couldn't afford to lose the rest of the column. But equally, he couldn't leave a sick man on this road, in this forest.

'Here.' He tried hauling Andersen to his feet, but the Swede was a big man and Phoenix was tugging uselessly at a dead weight. He knelt beside him in despair. 'There's got to be somebody,' he cried, his words echoing across the treetops, 'Anybody!'

And out there in the woods there was somebody. Somebody known to Phoenix. And he was coming.

'How did this happen?' groaned Phoenix. 'It couldn't have been any worse if it had been planned . . .' His voice trailed off.

Planned?

He looked around at the rain drumming on the webwork of tree roots and leaf-mould, then at the winding, empty forest track. Soon the approaching figure's footfalls would shake these tiny pools and rivulets.

Planned!

'Of course,' he said. 'This *was* planned. It's a trap.' He tugged feverishly at the scarf round Andersen's throat. The moment he saw the bite marks, the bat-shaped bruise, he fell backwards. Slowly, and without registering Phoenix, Andersen sat up. When he opened his mouth to gulp the chill air, there was no disguising the curved fangs.

He was changing, becoming a Vampyr.

'But it's daylight,' said Phoenix. 'You can't . . .'

'Oh, but he can,' came a voice behind him. 'Just as I can.'

'Adams!'

'I'm so glad you remembered me.'

The Vampyr who walked by daylight seemed even taller and more powerful than before.

'You see, Phoenix my old friend,' Adams said sneeringly. 'For very different reasons, both Andersen and I can walk abroad in daylight hours. I, you see, am no real Vampyr. As part of my apprenticeship, I am permitted to adopt the creature's more useful trappings. They are gifts from my master, I have its strength, its talons, its fangs. As for Andersen, blood was exchanged last night. At the moment, this tired, bewildered zombie is half-man, half-Vampyr. He isn't even aware of his part in my little plan. But by tonight he will have completed his transformation. Then he will be a soldier of the Legion, and he will never again feel the sunlight on his skin. There's a certain sadness in it, don't you agree?'

Phoenix was edging backwards, reaching for the Angel, hanging from his mount's saddle.

'Looking for this, Phoenix?' asked Adams, holding up the crossbow. 'Too late, I'm afraid.'

Phoenix felt for the axe in his belt.

'So,' said Adams, 'You feel like chopping some firewood, do you?' He uprooted a sturdy sapling from the roadside and hurled it in Phoenix's direction. 'Then cut away.'

Phoenix stared at the young tree at his feet. It would have taken two full-grown men half an hour to uproot it. Nervous sweat made the axe-handle slippery to hold.

'Scared?' asked Adams, stepping forward. 'Of course you are. But how scared? Scared to death? That's the easy kind of scared; the numbed, hopeless fear that makes the victim just lie down and die. But yours isn't like that, is it Phoenix? You're not like a lamb to the slaughter, at all. You're a fighter. You've still got hope. I know exactly what you're thinking. *Maybe I can get him with the axe. Or the stake. Maybe I can trick him. Maybe there is enough of the human left in Andersen to help me.*'

Phoenix winced. Every one of those thoughts had flashed through his mind.

'It's the hope that makes it worse,' said Adams. 'It makes the victim fight on long after any hope of escape has gone. It makes the kill long, and slow, and so, so painful.'

Phoenix felt the chatter of the points bracelet. His score was nearly down to zero.

'That's right, Phoenix,' said Adams. 'You're in the red zone now. So tell me, Legendeer . . .' He leaned forward, fangs bared.

'Are you ready to die?'

7

Lightning flashed far away, bluish light arcing over the densely packed trees. Phoenix heard thunder too, rolling through his head. Then he understood, it was the pounding of his own blood.

'What now, Phoenix?' asked Adams.

What now? I don't know.

'Do you stand and fight, or do you run?'

Phoenix stood facing Adams, feeling his old enemy towering over him, feeling his own weakness.

This is what I am. Nothing. And that's what his destiny was. Nothingness.

Seeing Phoenix rooted to the spot, the rain streaming over his face, Adams reached forward and picked up the tree trunk he had uprooted.

'This is no sport,' he said. 'All this time I have been waiting to settle accounts with you, and what do you do? Is this it? Is this the way I am to experience my victory? Are you really going to surrender so easily?'

Phoenix watched Adams wielding the tree like a club. 'What's happened to you, Adams?' He gave a bitter laugh. 'Do you know what's funny? Your mother actually thought I might have done something *to you*!'

For a split second he saw the shadow of emotion working in Adams' face, as if what was left of the teenage boy was trying to fight its way to the surface of the demon-apprentice who was advancing on him.

'You want to know what I'm going to do?' Phoenix asked,

shifting backwards. 'Well, I'm not going to lie down and die.'

His decision was made. Without the Angel, he was virtually unarmed. He turned and ran, his feet scrambling over the damp, sliding surface. Behind him, he heard a roar of triumph, then Adams making surprisingly agile progress through the trees. Horror flickered through Phoenix in cold needles. This creature he was facing wasn't the jealous, bullying boy he had encountered in Brownleigh. This was something else entirely, larger than life; stronger, quicker and more savage. Every time he leapt, Adams seemed to leap further, closing the distance between them. Every time he jinked, Adams seemed to do it faster, bringing himself closer to his quarry.

'Having fun, Phoenix? Enjoying our little game of cat and mouse?'

Phoenix plunged forward, branches whipping against his face. He tried to blot out Adams' voice, fixing his attention on the raindrops whispering through the forest canopy. Lightning flickered again through the glistening rain. As he ran, he even found his thoughts turning to his parents. He imagined them at the computer, willing him to run, to escape. But there was no escape, just the rain, the lightning and *him*, the remorseless hunter, never flagging, never tiring.

'This is good, Phoenix,' Adams chuckled. 'Very good.'

Phoenix wanted to turn and ram Adams' words down his throat. But that would be fatal. Flight was his only chance.

Chance. Chance of what?

It was hopeless. He had no weapon, no direction, no plan. All that was left to him was the will to survive.

To win.

But the effort to force himself on was almost more than he could bear. His breathing was coming in shallow, tortured gasps. He paused, clinging to an overhanging branch, and retched. He heard Adams behind him and threw himself forward. His left foot caught in a root and he rolled helplessly down a sudden, steep slope, the breath crashing out of him. As he rolled and somersaulted through the downpour he saw more light.

What Phoenix was seeing, bobbing through the waterlogged murk of the forest, were lanterns. Yes, lanterns and torches! Then he heard voices. Laura's voice. Then Ann's, Bird's Eye's, Bradshaw's.

'I'm here. Over here!'

Behind him, dark and lowering in the gloom, stood Adams. He had his head cocked, listening to the approaching voices.

'You've lost me, Adams,' yelled Phoenix, triumphant. 'Hear that? It's my friends.'

The Vampyr-hunters were running towards him, crossbows primed.

'The next time you see me, I'll be prepared. We're going to destroy you, Adams. You, Dracul and your master.' He was searching for his enemy, but he had lost him in the shadowy heart of the forest. 'Do you hear me? We're coming for you.'

But Adams had gone.

Ten minutes' walk brought them back to Dimitrescu's horsemen.

'You're safe,' said Dimitrescu.

'Yes,' said Bradshaw brightly. 'The lad's safe, all right. You won't believe it. There he was in the middle of a strange forest, hundreds of miles from home, and he was heading right for us.' He threw his arms wide. 'That's right, he found his way in this wilderness.'

'It's as if he had a compass,' said Ann.

'I did,' said Phoenix.

He tapped his forehead. 'It's in here.'

'This is all very interesting,' said Laura, who knew all about Phoenix's instinct. 'But I think we had better get moving.'

All around them night was falling.

8

There was no sunset that evening. Instead, the daylight began to surrender bit by bit, its frail glow gradually engulfed. Upon hearing Phoenix's story, Dimitrescu had hurriedly dispatched two riders to find Andersen, in the hope that his soul might still be rescued. It was something Phoenix was beginning to understand about fighters like Dimitrescu and Bradshaw. Behind their ruthlessness, there was a bond with everyone who took up arms against the undead. Even with somebody who had been bitten, their veins invaded by the contagion of Vampyrism. A few minutes after leaving, Dimitrescu's men returned with the Angel and two loose horses, but without Andersen.

'We have lost valuable time,' Dimitrescu said, devastated by the turn of events. 'This will set all our plans awry.'

'Plans?' Phoenix repeated. 'What plans are these?' He caught Laura's eye. It was his turn to be excluded from the group's decisions.

By way of a reply, Dimitrescu dismounted and wrenched back a corner of the tarpaulin covering the cart.

'Explosives!' cried Phoenix. 'Did you give permission for this, Foxton?'

Foxton nodded. 'It was our plan to deploy them after we reached Csespa. We thought that we would have a few hours of daylight to complete our work.' He glanced fearfully at the oncoming night. 'Now we have lost two hours. The storm slowed us down by well over an hour, and we lost a good thirty minutes looking for you. Young Robert was able to lead us into the general area of the forest, but that was all.'

Phoenix hung his head.

'No no, my boy. I meant to apportion no blame. It is simply a fact. None of us are to blame for the treacherous ways of the Vampyr. Circumstances have conspired to leave us stranded in this infernal forest.' He glanced at his fob watch. How long would it take us to reach Csespa, Nikolai?'

'At least another half hour.'

'Then we had better face facts. We are going to have to confront the demon hordes here, then fight our way through to the village.'

As if to confirm his words, a lone Wolver started to howl, its unearthly cry echoing across the mountains.

'Up there,' said Laura.

The silver beast was perched on top of a gaunt crag. Within seconds its mournful howling had been taken up at points all around them.

'What do you see, Robert?' asked Ann.

Bird's Eye was overwhelmed. 'Shadows,' he said, 'And shadows upon shadows. It's like a tidal wave, mother. So many, so many . . .'

Then the dimming sky was filled with shadowy figures. Dozen of them, Vampyrs on the wing, skimming across the heaped cloud like black kites.

'Get to it,' Bradshaw urged Dimitrescu. 'Unpack the explosives.'

The mountain track became a hotbed of activity as the Vampyr-hunters made their preparations. Sticks of explosive were strapped to arrows, stakes were hammered into the ground, braziers were lit in a circle around them. Then Bird's Eye was shouting, bawling at the top of his voice.

'It's starting. We're under attack!'

As ever, the Wolvers led the way, hurtling out of the darkness, rain spraying from their fur, their eyes flashing red, their mantrap jaws snapping. In response longbow arrow and crossbow bolt hissed and crunched, cutting a swathe through the attacking ranks. But, no matter how many fell, still more came on, roaring and howling, splintering the six-foot stakes like matchwood. In response the Szekelys thundered forward setting off explosions right at the heart of the Wolver charge. The night itself seemed on fire, the huge bodies of the demons lifted into the blazing sky.

'Retrieve what arrows you can from the bodies,' Dimitrescu ordered. 'The moment we slacken our fire, they will have us.'

Even as the defenders within the burning circle kept up their withering hail of fire, the noose was tightening. Vampyrs fell out of the sky, hideous shrieks bursting from their throats.

'Ramsay,' Ann asked, 'Did you ever see so many?'

Foxton shook his head. Fear had strangled the words right out of him. Shattering explosions continued to rip the darkness apart, but such was the mass of suckers and rippers swarming through the woods that the defensive positions were already being overrun. The night became a symphony of terror. The hiss of arrows mingled with the whipcrack of explosives and the hoarse shouts of the Szekelys, the shrieking of the Vampyrs, the howling of the Wolvers.

'Phoenix!' cried Laura. 'Behind you.'

Phoenix spun round but too late. A Vampyr was upon him, its talons shredding his jacket and raking his back. Only three thick layers of clothing saved him from a mortal wound. As he struggled against the vice-like grip of the sucker, Phoenix heard Adams' voice behind and above him. It was crackling with menace.

'Why fight?' he asked. 'Why torment yourselves?'

As Phoenix strained to hold off the gleaming fangs, he saw his enemy, standing on the very crag where he had seen the first Wolver.

'Why labour so to delay the inevitable?'

If he hadn't been in such a precarious state, barely holding the Vampyr three inches from his throat, Phoenix might have found Adams' words laughable. The inarticulate bully he had met only months before would never have spoken in this way. Transformation indeed!

'It's hopeless. The night is my domain.'

Your domain! But you're nothing.

Phoenix found his voice. 'You're just the Gamesmaster's lackey!'

'Lackey?' said Adams. 'Is that what you think? How wrong you are, Phoenix. I am the disciple. That makes me head of his Legions, heir to his power.'

Phoenix's senses reeled. Heir to his power. It couldn't be!

Rage gave him new strength and he grappled with the sucker, feeling in his belt for a stake. The terrible struggle resulted in the pair of them, youth and creature, falling heavily to the ground and rolling through the trees. As he tumbled through the downpour, jolting agonizingly over the rough ground, Phoenix glimpsed brief freeze-frames of the battle. He saw Sakarov wielding his bow like a club, desperate to hold off the onslaught of the demon that had been Andersen. He saw Foxton shooting bolts from his chair, flanked by Ann and Bird's Eye. He could just make out Bradshaw and the Szekelys trying to give some kind of shape and purpose to the madness of battle.

With a roar, Phoenix yanked the stake from his belt and plunged it into the ghoul's back, penetrating the heart from behind. The thrill of triumph only lasted a second. Barely had he felt the creature's hold slacken than he realized with horror that they were teetering on the edge of a steep rock face. The Vampyr was either dead or dying, but it was still clinging to him, its weight pulling him forward. Just as he felt his feet finally slip off the rock, he heard Laura's voice.

'Phoenix, no!'

Then he was falling, wind rushing up at him, towards the jagged boulders far below.

And all was blackness.

9

Craning forward as far as she dared, Laura gazed down into the gorge. She could make something out, a dark star against the bleached paleness of the rocks. That had to be them, or at least one of them. She wanted to shout down, to call to Phoenix that she was coming. But that would have been foolhardy . . . or useless. She stole a glance at Adams, who had been watching the course of the battle from his vantage point high on the exposed crag. He followed Phoenix's fall, then vanished from the spur.

I've got to reach him first, thought Laura, unnerved by Adams' disappearance.

She started to edge down the cliff. Once over the shelf of rock on which she had been crouching, she found to her relief that it wasn't as steep as she had at first thought. Still looking around for some sign of Adams, she scrambled down, bringing herself closer to the dark star below. She could still hear the sounds of the battle, but they were becoming muffled. Where there had been nothing but savagery and explosions, there was now only the dripping darkness. Laura felt guilty abandoning the fight, but she couldn't leave Phoenix down there, hurt . . . or worse.

'That's right,' she said under her breath, 'Steady does it. No risks.'

She felt every step of the way through the thin soles of her boots. But even this wary descent was not without its danger. Once she dislodged a chip of rock, sending it bouncing down the slope. She held her breath, but the dark star didn't move.

Down and down she climbed, barely daring to breathe, barely daring to look as the dark star came closer.

'Just a few more steps. Just a few more.'

Eventually she reached the bottom. The rain had stopped and the mood glided from behind the clouds, illuminating the ground at the bottom of the cliff. She saw the dark star close up. It was the Vampyr with which Phoenix had been fighting. It was lying spreadeagled over a boulder, and quite, quite dead.

But where was Phoenix?

All of a sudden, from a thicket to her left, there was movement. The shaking of the branches set off a flush of gladness in her chest. She was tempted to rush forward. An instant later, she was thankful she hadn't. Red eyes raked the night.

Wolver!

She heard the snuffling, snarling approach. No doubt about it. There was a ripper among the small fir saplings not ten yards away.

Please, no!

She flattened herself against the ground, feeling the damp and cold strike up through her dress. Her breath was being shaken out of her by the relentless banging of her heart. Then she saw it. Not the whole creature, not tail, legs, head, fangs. Just a silver-grey blur. A scrap of wolf-demon shifting across the edge of her vision. The thought flared fire-bright in her brain:

It's seen me! She pressed her face into the mossy earth, as if trying to bury herself. What was it doing? She found herself making a list of really stupid instructions: Stay still. Don't breathe. And if you have to . . . do it quietly! The silence weighed heavily. It began to crush her. She wanted to look up from the sodden ground, but she didn't dare. Then she heard it shifting.

Can you see me?

But the beast didn't need to see. It smelt girl and it smelt fear. It knew who she was and what she was feeling.

So why don't you strike? Trying to suck the breath deep down inside her she turned her eyes towards it. Then she understood. Midway between the spot where she was lying and the Wolver lay Phoenix.

You're guarding him.

Lifting her head, Laura saw Adams making his way down the cliff. He was coming to retrieve his trophy. She wanted to rush over and shake Phoenix awake and warn him, but the Wolver gave a low, throaty growl, a kind of rumble that drummed over the chilly gooseflesh on her arms.

He's alive, she thought, looking at Phoenix lying face down. He has to be. Why guard a dead boy?

She had to act, but how? She could feel the weight of her crossbow, slung over her back. There was a single quarrel primed in the slot. It posed an agonizing dilemma.

Two demons, one shot.

She could taste her own fear, thick and pungent in her throat. And the low, inhuman rumble came again, rising steadily into a nerve-shredding whine and finally the eerie, moon-born howl of the Wolver.

'Get away from him!'

Laura was on her feet, crossbow in her hands, pointing it first at the ripper than at Adams.

'What the matter, Laura?' he asked. 'Spoilt for choice?'

Then the silver-grey fur and the snakk-snakk-snakking mantrap jaws were fused together in a terrifying primal rage. Laura squeezed the crossbow trigger. The ripping never came. Instead there was a scream, half-animal, half-human and the silver-grey killing machine kicking, yelping . . . and dying.

'Excellent shot,' said Adams, as he reached the floor of the gorge. 'But now what?' He drew the bolt from the Wolver's body and snapped it in pieces. 'A successful kill, but it has left you completely unarmed.' He started to walk towards her. 'At long last,' he said. 'I have you both. You've led my master a merry dance. Now I do believe the game is over.'

'Get back . . . Don't you dare come near me . . . Keep

away.' Her words were coming out in gasps; angry, frightened sobs of helpless rage.

'It's all over, Laura,' said Adams, reaching out.

But it wasn't. Just as his talons were brushing her cheeks, he stiffened. Then his hands began to tremble wildly. One hand flew to his shoulder blades. A moment later, he was staring down in disbelief at the crossbow bolt he had drawn out.

'Oh, it's over all right,' said Phoenix. 'But not the way you thought.'

As Adams sank to the ground, Phoenix reloaded and aimed. Laura was about to protest. Not like this, not in cold blood. But it never came to negotiation with Phoenix. She was about to speak when she saw something swooping, kite-black and hissing.

'Phoenix, behind you!'

He dropped to one knee, turned and shot. The swoop of the Vampyr ended with the airy song of the Angel. The moment's respite was all Adams needed. The sucker had given him a way out. Staggering from his wound, he plunged into the black depths of the woods. Phoenix made as if to set off in pursuit, but Laura grabbed his sleeve.

'We'll never find him in there,' she said.

'We've got to. This will never be over while he lives.'

'If you go in after him, you'll be killed. Imagine how many demons are in there. Besides, you've seen his powers of recovery.'

Phoenix hesitated.

'Is that what you want? To throw your life away?'

Phoenix consulted the points bracelet. His score was healthy. The hesitation became resolve. 'No,' said Phoenix. 'Let's climb back up and see how the battle went.'

So they started to climb, every step full of hope, and dread.

10

Laura looked around the mountain track. 'Where is everybody?'

There was evidence enough of a struggle. The earth was gouged by the hooves of the horses and pitted by dynamite blasts. Bolts and arrows stuck up out of the ground and from the trunks of the trees, like pins from a cushion. The braziers had burned low but still cast an eerie glow over the battleground. But of Wolvers and Vampyrs and their beleaguered opponents there was no sign. Not a single body lay on the churned earth.

'Phoenix,' Laura asked anxiously. 'Is this good news, or bad?'

Phoenix shook his head, willing the ploughed ground to give up its secrets. 'I don't know what to think.'

Another inspection of the area yielded a find. Phoenix picked up the wooden effigy Dimitrescu had been given at Constanta.

'A lot of good this did us,' he said.

Laura cupped her hands, and was about to call out.

'What do you think you're doing?' snapped Phoenix.

'I was going to call for help.'

'And what if our people lost?' Phoenix said. 'What if they're all gone? You would be bringing the demons down on our heads.'

'Sorry.'

After a moment or two his tense face relaxed, and he smiled. 'It's all right. I know you're scared. So am I. But we have to think. We've got to get to Csespa Castle. It's the key to everything.'

'But what can we do, just the two of us?'

Phoenix shrugged. 'Whatever we can.' He spent a few minutes retrieving crossbow bolts, then walked along the track a way. 'Laura,' he hissed, 'Come here.' He pointed ahead, indicating hoofprints and the twin furrows cut by the wheels of a cart or a carriage.

'They're alive!' Laura exclaimed.

'Either that,' said Phoenix cautiously, 'or the demons took the horses and transport.'

'I wish you hadn't said that.'

A great, unnatural silence had settled over the forest. The only sound came from the raindrops tapping off the branches.

'Keep to the side of the track,' said Phoenix, 'Out of the moonlight.'

There was a shiver in the mountain breeze, a nervous, unsettling cold that had the pair of them starting out of their skins at the slightest movement in the woods. After a few minutes Phoenix felt Laura close by him. She linked her arm through his and they walked on, huddled together. After over half an hour Phoenix was almost sleep-walking, trudging along like a robot, his eyes half-closed with exhaustion. For some reason, tired as he was, he couldn't bring himself to put down the wooden effigy. It was a link with their comrades.

All of a sudden Laura pulled her arm from his.

'What is it?'

'Up there!'

She was slightly ahead of him, pointing excitedly. 'The castle.'

It was just as Foxton had described it, jutting abruptly out of the mountain top on which it perched. The huge stone pile was marked by walled outworks, into which there were carved tiny slits of windows. The entire dizzily rising edifice was topped by red-tiled turrets and towers. Any entrance was hidden by the tangle of fir and spruce that seemed to claw half way up the sheet walls.

'Journey's end,' said Phoenix.

'So what do we do now?' asked Laura.

'I know what we don't do,' Phoenix answered. 'We don't go near the castle while it's still dark.'

Laura smiled. 'Who's arguing?'

It was another fifteen or twenty minutes before their lonely trek ended. They found a rough, wooden hut. There was no furniture and it was barely possible for even one person to lie down. It hardly mattered. Phoenix was so tired he used the effigy, wrapped up in his coat, as a kind of pillow. Even sitting up in their damp clothes, they were soon fast asleep.

Phoenix was being shaken awake. Through barely parted eyelids he saw the pinched, bearded face of a man in his late sixties or early seventies looking down at him. A stream of incomprehensible words came from his lips.

'I'm sorry,' said Phoenix. 'I don't understand.'

Laura was also awake. 'Maybe he thinks we're trespassing.'

Another torrent of gruff Romanian followed.

'It's no good,' said Phoenix, holding out both hands, 'We don't understand.' He stood up to make his point. 'We come from England.' As he rose to his feet, the effigy slipped from behind him. The peasant's eyes widened. One word Phoenix recognized:

'*Moroi.*'

'Yes,' he said, keen to reassure the man. 'We're Vampyr-hunters.' He realized how stupid that must sound coming from two teenagers, but the peasant wasn't interested in what they looked like, only the strange, wooden carving.

'*Moroi.*'

'That's right,' said Phoenix, sounding like something from a 1950s farce. 'Here. Lots of *moroi*.' Then the man was backing away, ashen-faced.

'You don't need to go,' said Laura soothingly. 'We come to

141

help.' But the peasant had seen enough. Retreating into the thin morning sunlight, he started to run.

'Come back,' shouted Phoenix. 'Please.' But he was gone, snapping twigs and trembling branches the only clue to his path.

'Whatever that thing is,' Laura said, remembering the tavern at Buzau, 'it scares the hell out of the locals.'

Phoenix picked it up and stared through the trees at the walls of the castle. 'Let's just hope it does the same to Vampyrs.'

'You mean we're going up there?'

'That's right.'

'But shouldn't we find the others?'

Phoenix stared at the ground. 'What others? You saw his face. We're the first strangers he'd seen. That seals it for me. They didn't get through.'

'Oh no.' Laura sank to the ground.

'And where's Adams?' said Phoenix. 'You can be sure he's up to something. Maybe he's up there right now, preparing our reception party.'

Laura hugged herself, as if suddenly chilled to the bone.

'From here on in,' said Phoenix. 'We're all on our own.'

11

The castle wasn't approached by a drawbridge, but by a narrow, paved walkway, cut out of the rock on which it stood. To either side, over the low walls, Phoenix and Laura could gaze down the dizzying drop.

'That's where Dracul threw Foxton,' said Phoenix.

They didn't look down too often, preferring to keep their eyes straight ahead. Neither of them was over-fond of heights. From their raised vantage point they could see the hamlet of Csespa itself, nestling among the spruce trees. At this distance it seemed impossibly pretty, a picture-postcard view of central Europe. But they both knew what the picturesque vista hid – a history stained in blood and a population living in terror.

'Do you think this is wise?' Laura asked as they approached the thick, iron-plated wooden door at the end of the walkway. It stood ajar like the half-open jaws of a sleeping reptile. Phoenix rested the Angel in the crook of his arm.

'No,' he said, 'I'm sure it isn't, but wisdom and caution don't really come into it. We're all that's left of our mission. We've got no choice.' They eased their way through the gateway, looking up at the huge barbican. 'At least nobody is pouring boiling oil down on us.'

Laura crouched protectively. 'That isn't funny.'

Once through the gateway, they found themselves in a huge square, confronting the irregular jumble of buildings that made up the central complex of the castle. The dirt-grimed panes of glass set deep into the stone were hardly like windows. They gave the outsider no view into the building and would afford precious little to anyone on the inside trying to look out. The paint on the window frames was peeling and yellowish. Phoenix stepped back, raising his eyes to the upper storeys.

'He's in there somewhere,' he said.

Laura nodded. 'That's what I'm afraid of.'

Phoenix gave a half-smile. 'Come on, we've work to do. You know what we're looking for: a room with an exit, but no entrance.'

Laura followed him up to the front door of what must once have been living quarters. As Phoenix turned the handle, she started to wish it was locked, but with a creaking noise the door gave and yawned open. 'Ugh, that smell.' They recognized it immediately, the stench of decay. The perfume of the living dead. 'This is his lair, all right.'

The high ceilings were a lattice-work of cracks and many of the walls sported brown damp patches, while the patterned carpet beneath their feet had faded almost beyond recognition. The furniture too sported the patina of age. The whole place, in short, reeked of neglect. Phoenix took a few steps inside, then paused, looking down one of the murky galleries that ran to left and right. When Laura followed him, she took the precaution of slipping a bolt into her crossbow. Phoenix had been about to remark on the quiet inside the house, but the words didn't come. The door had slammed shut behind them.

From then on it wasn't the silence, but the amount of noise that began to strike him. There was nothing loud, just a slow, stealing chorus creeping through the dank air. Woodwork snapped and clicked, floorboards creaked, window frames rattled and somewhere deep within the maze of passages the wind whistled. There was something else too. The daylight itself seemed lost in the great gloom of the castle. It was like a guttering candle on the brink of extinction.

'What a foul place!' said Laura.

'Did you expect anything else?' asked Phoenix. They moved forward uncertainly.

'Which way?' asked Laura, 'And don't you dare say we're going to split up. I never know why they do that in the movies.'

'We're going to search the place room by room,' said Phoenix. 'Stay close and only speak when it's really necessary.'

They took one of the long galleries, inspecting every room, alcove and recess. In some of the rooms they found oil lamps or candlesticks, but not one was ever lit. The entire collection of rooms was a temple of half-light. After an hour of exploring the oak-panelled corridors, they found themselves back in the main hall, facing the great staircase.

'I suppose that means it's upstairs next,' said Laura.

Phoenix led the way, listening to each stair creak protestingly as he climbed. At the top of the staircase there was a huge oil-painting. The figure it depicted was wearing battle-dress, possibly late Middle Ages. He wore his hair long. But what distinguished him were his piercing eyes, very dark and very hard.

'That's him, isn't it?'

'Dracul. Yes, it could well be.'

The eyes were fiery and there was a definite reddish hue to the long hair. While they looked at it a deep moan seemed to steal through the house. Now they could put a face to Dracul, but what of the menace lurking behind, the Gamesmaster himself?

'Did you hear a voice?' asked Phoenix.

'I heard *something*.' Though it wasn't yet noon, they were speaking in hushed tones as if it were blackest night.

'Which way now?'

The green-tinted passageways to left and right looked identical, but Phoenix was determined not to show indecision. He struck out to the left, and all the way he heard the sounds of the castle's macabre inner life. What Phoenix had mistakenly taken for silence when they had first entered was something else entirely. There were a whole range of barely audible noises. Though muffled, they were definitely there, the sounds of scratching and scraping, a dull thud almost like a heartbeat, the grinding of something being dragged along a floor above their heads.

'Do you hear that?' asked Laura. 'The whole place is alive.' Like a maggoty corpse, the corruption seething just beneath the skin.

'I know.'

Again and again they looked into rooms, but every time they were empty. What's more, they all had entrances and exits, doors and windows.

'This is hopeless,' said Laura.

'We keep going,' insisted Phoenix. 'It's here somewhere. It's got to be.'

So on they went, from one room to the next, the belief growing that they were chasing shadows. It was halfway down yet another identical passageway that Laura stopped suddenly. 'Did you hear something?'

'I've been hearing things ever since we entered.'

'No, this is different. Not a little sound,' said Laura. 'Something else.' The words were hardly out of her mouth, when there was a crash, like a pane of glass being smashed in.

'You're right,' said Phoenix. 'We're not alone in here.'

12

He stood rooted to the spot listening.

'Adams?' Laura asked.

'He's the only demon who walks by daylight,' said Phoenix. His arms and legs felt heavy, his body a patchwork of tiredness and pain. For the first time he remembered that he hadn't eaten and became aware of the gnawing at his stomach. He feared the demon he didn't know, the waiting Dracul. But one thing more than any other added to the aching tiredness, and that was the knowledge that Adams was close by. And he was stronger, quicker, more completely ruthless than Phoenix would ever be.

I don't want to fight him again.

'Phoenix, are you all right?'

'Don't worry about me, I'm . . .' His voice choked off. A split-second after he had started speaking, he had heard somebody moving somewhere in the depths of the castle. The sound was more distinct this time, the regular beat of footfalls on the stairs. The expression on Laura's face confirmed that she had heard it too. 'It's closer,' said Phoenix, lowering his voice to a whisper.

They edged towards the stairwell, darting nervous glances at each other. Laura caught sight of movement below them and shrank back, flattening herself against the wall.

'Who is it? *What* is it?'

Phoenix craned over the wooden rail, trying to see. 'Aim for the top of the stairs,' he hissed, scurrying over to a wooden chest, which he used for cover.

147

Through the larger windows that lit the galleries on the east side of the castle, Phoenix could see the wind-swept mountainside and the blanket of fir and spruce. For a moment he thought he saw shadowy movement. Maybe it was people moving up towards them, but a moment later there was no sign of them at all.

Now I'm seeing things.

He waved gently to Laura, signalling the best he could that she should hang fire. Laura gave a nervous thumbs up and looked down the stock of the crossbow, taking careful aim. At last the cause of their anxiety came into view. Phoenix's finger had been stroking the crossbow trigger, itching to shoot. It didn't come to that. With an overwhelming sense of relief, he took his hand away.

'Bird's Eye!'

'You're alive!' cried Laura. 'What about the others? Where are they?'

Bird's Eye sat down heavily on a window-seat. 'I thought I would never catch up with you.'

'How did you get away? Where have you been?'

Bird's Eye took a deep breath, then started to tell his story: 'We were being overrun. I don't know exactly when you two vanished into the night, but the fight was chaos. The demons were in amongst us. We couldn't use bows for fear of hitting one another. It was terrifying. I'm not sure how I got separated from the others. One minute Bradshaw and my mother were right beside me, the next I had two Wolvers on my heels. They chased me into the woods. I was fleeing for my life, when one of Dimitrescu's men appeared out of nowhere. He slew one of the Wolvers, but the second was too quick. He gave his life saving mine. I recovered myself enough to kill the second Wolver, but by the time I got back to the track, everyone had gone.'

'Any idea where they are?'

'I don't know. At least some of them are alive. I see their shadows, but faintly. I can't make out faces. I've been on my own for hours.'

'So how did you get here?'

'I don't really know. I must have walked most of the night. I probably went round and round in circles. In the end I couldn't walk any more and got what sleep I could at the roadside. I just huddled under my cape and lay there. I've never been so cold, or so alone. Shortly after dawn I started following the most obvious landmark, hoping to find survivors.'

'You headed for the castle?'

Bird's Eye nodded. 'I had a vision. It led me up here. That's when I saw the two of you. You were a good distance ahead of me, making your way across the walkway into the castle. I followed you, of course. The door was locked. I had to smash a window to get in.'

'The door was locked, you say?'

'That's right.'

Phoenix and Laura exchanged glances.

So who locked it?

'When I got inside I couldn't find you. I didn't dare call to you. I didn't know what else might be moving about in here. I'd just about given up hope of finding you.'

'It's good to see you too,' said Laura. 'You must have been so scared.' Bird's Eye was close to tears.

'We've been looking for the room you told us about,' Phoenix told him. 'The one with an exit but no entrance. We've drawn a blank so far.'

'It won't be in this part of the castle,' said Bird's Eye. 'It can't be. The sight came to me again on my way up here. The room I saw is high up, *really* high. In my vision I could make out the ground a long way below. It wasn't even a room to be honest, more of a large recess in the castle wall.'

'Higher up?' said Laura. 'Then it's got to be one of the towers.'

They were about to head for the front door when they became aware of a change in the brooding house. All the small creaking, scuttering sounds seemed to be coming together in one ominous rush of noise. It was like a tidal wave breaking, and it was coming towards them.

'What is that?' Phoenix couldn't place the sound, but it was rising in volume. It reminded him of rainfall, but it crackled with menace. He imagined a blizzard of autumn leaves, but it was infinitely more threatening. 'Bird's Eye?'

'I see a brown tide. It's on the ceiling and on the walls.' Laura ran to the top of the stairs, and screamed.

Bird's Eye put his hand to his mouth, as if he was about to be sick. 'Cockroaches. I see a flood of vermin.' Which was exactly what was sweeping towards them.

'This way.' Phoenix led them into a gallery they had not explored, but it was the same story there. They could see the brown carapaces of thousands of insects coating the floor, walls and ceilings, turning the passageway into a heaving, chattering tunnel.

'What do we do?' cried Phoenix.

Laura was tearing at her face. 'Get me out of here,' she pleaded. 'I can't bear the things. Not on my skin, not touching me.' The noise was now deafening, drilling into their brains.

'It's no good,' said Phoenix. 'I can't think.'

Nor could Bird's Eye, but he could see. 'Here.' He was pointing to a small recess in the shadows. 'This is our way out.'

Phoenix pulled a flashlight from his belt and trained the beam into the recess. He highlighted a wooden panel. 'Stand back.'

Laura was holding her ears, trying to blot out the rustling approach of the insects. 'Hurry.'

Phoenix used the stock of the Angel like a hammer. The panel started to splinter. 'It's giving.'

'Hurry!'

Phoenix kicked in the remainder of the panel. 'What's down there?' he asked Bird's Eye.

'I can't help you,' came the worrying reply. 'All I see is darkness.' The carpet of insects had almost reached them.

'We've no choice anyway,' said Phoenix, 'Follow me down.'

With that, he dived into the void. At the end of the dizzying drop he found himself crawling across a stone-tiled floor. 'Laura, Bird's Eye.' For several agonizing moments, there was no answer. Then he heard Laura's voice somewhere to his left.

'Where Bird's Eye?'

'I'm over here. I think I've found the way out.'

13

They emerged through a small hatch, low down in the castle wall. Outside, the sky was beginning to grow darker, flakes of snow swirling in the gusting wind. The air had become bitterly cold, slicing through clothing and snipping at skin.

'I'm not sure this is any better than indoors,' said Laura, shuddering.

'Don't worry,' said Phoenix, gazing up at the tallest of the castle's towers. 'We'll be inside again soon enough.'

Bird's Eye was walking slowly backwards, never looking away from the tower. 'This is the one,' he said, 'I can feel it.' Then it was as if he were up there, shivering against the wind's blasts, and looking down at the ground below. He cried out and staggered, clinging to Phoenix for support.

'What is it?'

'I was up there,' Bird's Eye replied. 'I was looking down at you.'

'Where from?' Phoenix demanded. 'Which window?'

Still hanging onto Phoenix, Bird's Eye pointed upwards, at an opening just below the top of the tower. 'There.' What Bird's Eye had indicated was a windowless opening in the rock. Strangely, it reminded him of an old man's mouth.

'I'm going up. Who's with me?'

'Not me,' said Bird's Eye. 'Not up there.'

Phoenix smiled. 'That's all right. We need you down here to point it out.'

'I suppose that means I'm coming with you,' said Laura.

'You must. I need somebody to cover me.'

Phoenix led the way to the rotten wooden door at the foot of the tower. Pausing for a moment to look at the dark mass of drifting snow-cloud, he stepped into the gloom. He pulled a torch from his belt and started up the winding stone steps. They had been climbing for a few minutes when Laura yelped.

'Sorry,' she said when Phoenix looked round, 'Cobwebs.'

'Honestly,' he said, 'You and creepy-crawlies.'

She wasn't going to take that. 'Those roaches freaked you out too, remember.' A few more minutes into their climb, and they came to a door.

'Do you think it's the one?' asked Laura.

'Hardly. We can't be more than half-way up. I just want to get my bearings.' Phoenix crossed the straw-littered floor to the window. It was barred. 'Won't open,' he grumbled. 'I can't get Bird's Eye's attention.'

Behind him, Laura was wondering out loud: 'What was this place for, do you think?'

Phoenix jerked a thumb at a dark recess. 'See for yourself.'

Laura registered the skeleton and the manacles hanging loosely from its fleshless wrists. 'Ugh, let's get out of here.'

The higher they went the more aware they became of the howling wind. At this height, the storm was raging with unimaginable ferocity like a colossus tearing at the stone walls. They examined several rooms before they reached one whose window they could open.

'Bird's Eye,' Phoenix yelled. 'How far?'

But Bird's Eye couldn't hear him. Phoenix's voice was being swallowed up by the roaring wind. He leaned further out, where the hailstones stabbed at his face.

'Bird's Eye!' Again there was no response.

'I know.' Phoenix pointed his torch at Bird's Eye. Bird's Eye immediately started skipping up and down and gesturing towards a point somewhere above his head. He was holding up two fingers.

'It's the second window up,' Phoenix declared triumphantly. 'Come on.' But they were in for a disappointment. From the tower's uppermost window they could look down on the opening. When they went down to the door below the opening was above them. 'So that's what Bird's Eye meant,' said Phoenix. 'The room has been walled up. Maybe it never had a door at all.'

'How could that be?' asked Laura.

Phoenix shook his head. 'All I know is this,' he said. 'We've got to find a way in.' But no matter how they searched, there was no sign of a secret door, or of loosened stones, nothing that might give them access to the room. Phoenix pounded a couple of steel tent pegs into the masonry, but it had little effect. 'At least we've marked the spot,' he said. Utterly discouraged, they started the long climb down to the ground. When they eventually opened the door and stepped back out into the strengthening wind, they couldn't see Bird's Eye.

'Where is he? Bird's Eye?' Fear knotted Phoenix's insides. 'Bird's Eye!'

'Phoenix, Laura, over here.'

They ran towards his voice. For once, it was good news.

'Dimitrescu! Bradshaw!'

Bird's Eye saved his greeting for somebody far more important. 'Mother!'

Led by Dimitrescu's horseman, the column were making their way up the hillside.

'Robert, thank goodness you're all right.'

'Does this mean you won the battle?' Phoenix asked.

'Aye,' Bradshaw replied. 'We won. But at a cost.'

'Six of my men,' said Dimitrescu sadly. 'And Sakarov. All dead.'

'But where have you been?'

'Down there,' said Bradshaw. 'In those endless woods. We were searching for you three. In the end we gave up hope and sought shelter in the village. We never dreamed you would be foolhardy enough to come up here. Not on your own.'

'Then my father spotted a light shining from the great tower,' said Dimitrescu.

154

'Your father?' An old man appeared from the back of the group. It was the peasant they had met in the hut that morning. 'You mean?'

'This is my village,' said Dimitrescu. 'I left as a young man, disgusted by their lack of fight. I returned twice, once to fight alongside Foxton and Van Helsing, once last year when my mother died.'

'But how did you know we were up here?' asked Laura.

Bradshaw answered that one. 'It was when old Dimitrescu told us about the youngsters he had disturbed this morning that we realized who was up here. Did you find anything?'

Bird's Eye pointed to the opening. 'That's the room, but there is no door. We searched high and low.'

'So the only way in is from the outside?' asked Ann. Phoenix nodded.

'Well, there will be no scaling the tower in this storm,' said Bradshaw, squinting against the blizzard. 'We will defend our position in the village and return tomorrow.'

Phoenix took one last look at the tower.

Until tomorrow.

14

It was during the late afternoon of that day, as the snow fell heavily and the wind clawed at the walls, that Phoenix found himself thinking. Sitting by the fireside in the Dimitrescu household, dipping small pieces of bread in his bowl of soup, he thought of his parents. He thought of them as Laura had so often thought of her own mother and father. He had seen the look on her face. The longing to be home. But at least Laura's parents were spared knowing what was happening in this other world. Frozen in a single moment in time, they didn't have to watch their daughter fighting for her life. For Christina and John Graves it was different. They were spectators at an electronic Colosseum. He knew they were there at that very moment, watching. Always watching.

'Are you all right, Phoenix?' asked Ann, seeing the faraway look.

'Yes, just thinking.' He caught Laura's eye. There was a flash of understanding.

'It's almost dark,' said Ann. 'We'll have to go.'

With a sigh, Phoenix got up from his stool and put his bowl on the bare wooden table. It wasn't just Mum and Dad. There were other thoughts spinning in his mind, of the room with an exit but no entrance, of the gateway, and of the trinity of evil that stood in their way. If the battle was won tonight and the weather was kind tomorrow, it might be just a matter of hours before he finally came one step closer to defeating *him*, the owner of eyes that burned through the worlds.

The Gamesmaster.

'I'm ready,' he said.

As he trudged through the deep snow after Laura and the Van Helsings, Phoenix saw the stream of villagers heading for the church, responding to the urgent tolling of its bell. It was Dimitrescu's plan, to gather the entire population and defend a building which could hold them all.

'Look,' said Laura. 'You wouldn't think it was a church, would you?' She was right. The building had the appearance of a small fortress. Every window had been boarded up and crossbowmen were posted in the bell tower. The walls and the surrounding snowdrifts were stained by a crimson sunset.

As if with blood.

They had almost reached the low stone wall around the church, when Bird's Eye drew back sharply.

'What's the matter, Robert?' asked Ann.

'The suckers,' he gasped. 'They're already here.'

'Here?' They stood, peering into the Transylvanian dusk. They were being buffeted by the crowds of villagers, desperate to be inside.

'Bird's Eye,' Phoenix asked, 'What do you mean *here*?'

'I can see them, in the darkness.' He raised his face to the sky where the moon would soon be rising. 'They're moving, reaching up towards the moonlight.'

Phoenix frowned.

Reaching up. But from where? Then he saw it.

'The graveyard. Of course, they're in the graveyard. That's why the castle was so empty. They're *here*.'

A few families were making their way past the gravestones, glancing fearfully at the encroaching darkness. They obviously understood better than any outsider that this was a place of the undead.

'Get away from there!' Phoenix yelled. Then the words came, the only words he knew that they would understand: '*Moroi, strigoi.*'

But one man had taken a step too close to the graves.

Phoenix saw the earth erupting beneath his feet and a taloned hand reach up out of the soil and grasp his ankle.

'I'm coming. Laura, Ann, get those people into the church. Quick!' He ran to the stone wall, hurdling it with ease, and raced up the path to where the unfortunate man was already buried up to the waist. Two pairs of clawed hands were clinging to him, tearing at him, while unearthly shrieks bubbled up out of the earth.

'Give me your hand.' There was a look of confusion on the man's face. Phoenix reached out. 'Your hand. Now!' Gripping the man's wrist with one hand, Phoenix shot a bolt with the other. Then he was hacking at the exploding earth with the hatchet. Suddenly the man catapulted out of the demons' grasp and half-ran, half-crawled towards the relative safety of the church.

'Phoenix,' came Laura's voice. 'Run!' Soil-grimed Vampyrs were bursting from every grave, squealing like enraged beasts. From the bell tower and from slits in the boarded-up windows came a hail of crossbow quarrels, thudding into the suckers as they rose. Ducking under the flight of the arrows, Phoenix raced for the church. He was almost there when a Wolver came careering round the back of the church. He heard shouts of *pricolici*! Phoenix instinctively pressed the Angel's trigger but it clicked uselessly. He hadn't had a chance to reload. Only Ann's reactions saved him. She dashed forward, rested the stock of her bow on Phoenix's shoulder and shot into the creature's heart.

'Get inside,' Foxton was shouting from the church doorway. 'Hurry.' No sooner was the door locked, bolted and barred than a hurricane of fangs and claws fell upon the church. Above the din, a pounding could be heard from the roof.

'The bell tower,' said Bradshaw. 'Get those men down.' The bowmen were out of arrows and came spilling down the ladder, before turning and securing the hatch through which they had come. Phoenix heard them shouting breathless reports. He didn't understand the words, but he got the drift. The Legion was attacking in force.

'Why weren't people told to go to the village hall?' Phoenix asked angrily. 'Surely Dimitrescu knew the danger, the church being so close to the graveyard.' He looked around. 'Where is he, anyway? Where are the Szekelys?' He remembered the inn at Buzau and sought out Bradshaw. 'There's a plan, isn't there?'

Bradshaw lowered his crossbow and gestured to Laura to take his place at the window. 'Come with me.' He led Phoenix up to a pulpit. 'Look through here.'

Phoenix pressed his eye to a hole drilled through the heavy boarding. A force of fifty horsemen was flooding out of the village hall, launching fiery arrows into the night.

'But where did all those men come from?' asked Phoenix.

'Where do you think?' Bradshaw growled. 'Nikolai finally persuaded the villagers to fight. It's not a minute too soon, either.'

The Wolvers were cannoning repeatedly into the church's west wall. Already cracks were appearing and plaster was falling in lumps, showering people with dust. Phoenix and Bradshaw ran to reinforce the bowmen at the windows. The demons had ripped away most of the boarding by now and were reaching through the windows. Everybody, even the children, were striking back with anything to hand. They fought with spades, pitchforks, scythes, anything to keep the ghoulish tide at bay.

'Why don't they use the explosive again?' asked Phoenix, shooting into the throat of a bleach-faced sucker.

'We've got plans for it,' said Bradshaw. 'There isn't a stick to spare.'

Phoenix gave him a quizzical look, but it was no time for a question-and-answer session. Two Vampyrs had over-whelmed the defenders at a window just above the altar and were inside the building. Ann and Phoenix were the first to respond, bringing them down with quick, accurate shots.

Suddenly, the shrieking and howling outside reached fever pitch.

'It's the Szekelys,' said Bradshaw. He reached down the aisle, recruiting anybody who looked capable of fighting, putting together a force to go out and help Dimitrescu's commando. Phoenix elbowed his way to the front.

'Open the doors . . . now!' The moment Bradshaw's group was out, the great door slammed shut behind them. Out in the rush of the wind, Phoenix could see the size of the task facing them. There were still dozens of rippers and suckers pounding the outer walls of the church. But the odds were no longer impossible. Ghouls had stopped swarming up out of the graveyard and the skies were clear of Vampyrs.

The tide was turning.

15

The Legion came twice more before dawn broke over Csespa, but neither attack had the titanic force of that first onslaught.

'We've done it,' said Ann, as the demon tide receded into the lightening sky just before daybreak. 'We've fought them off.'

Foxton wiped the dust and sweat from his face, and turned his wheelchair in her direction. 'Yes, we've won this round. Get some sleep. We'll be on the move again later today.'

'So soon?' asked Ann.

Phoenix cut in: 'It's the castle, isn't it? We're going back to the castle.'

Foxton smiled wearily. 'Of course it's the castle. It's the fount of terror, and your path home. There we will find both the dark and the light sides of our world. We're going to burn Dracul out of his lair. This time he must perish.'

By the time Phoenix woke from his restless sleep, the first party had already been dispatched to the castle. Bradshaw and Dimitrescu were its leaders. Phoenix joined Foxton in his carriage.

'What are they doing up there?' he asked. 'I think I've a right to know.'

Foxton smiled at Laura climbing up after Phoenix, then addressed him: 'We're going to burn out the nest for good and all,' he explained. 'They're laying dynamite in as many rooms as they can. What they can't blow up, they plan to burn. Never in my sixty years have I been so close to victory.'

Panic took hold of Phoenix.

'Blow it up! But why wasn't this discussed? There should have been a meeting of the Committee.'

'There is no Committee,' said Foxton. 'Half our number are dead. All decisions have been taken by Bradshaw and Dimitrescu and myself. There can be no delay. Even now, after everything we have done, Dracul's power isn't broken. He is up there, waiting for us. We have to destroy his lair before night falls. But don't worry, my young friend, the fuse will not be lit until you have been given the chance to unlock the secret of the room. As you have made it clear many times, this is more than just a Vampyr plague.'

It was Laura's turn to be anxious. 'But what if we don't unlock its secret? You can't just go ahead regardless. Don't you understand, Mr Foxton? It's our only way home. We could be trapped here forever.'

'I'm sorry,' said Foxton as the carriage started to roll, 'You must understand our situation. We have broken the back of Vampyr power, but they can make more of the dead, an endless multiplication of terror. A single Vampyr can be the germ from which a new epidemic flourishes. We cannot allow them to recover, and spread their contagion anew. This has to be the death-blow. You will be given your chance to return home.' He consulted his fob watch. 'It is two o'clock. Darkness falls in two and a half hours. The remaining hours of daylight are your time. But, no matter what the result of your efforts, by nightfall this day Csespa castle must be destroyed.'

As the shuddering carriage moved out of the village, the inhabitants lined the route. They stood grim-faced and unsmiling, watching the second group of Vampyr-hunters depart.

'You'd think we'd lost,' Laura said. 'Just look at their faces.'

'These people have witnessed many false dawns,' Foxton told her. 'They have paid a terrible price for living in the shadow of the Vampyr. There will be no rejoicing until every one of the hell-fiends is destroyed.'

Phoenix looked out of the window, craning to catch a

glimpse of the castle. His destiny awaited him up there in that dark tower. The blood was pounding in his ears, every inch of his skin prickling with a mixture of fright and expectation. Why hadn't the Gamesmaster done more to stop them? Where was Adams? It could only mean one thing. The tower was their greatest challenge yet.

There's more to come, isn't there?

It was a bright day, crisp and still. The snowfall of the previous night lay banked to either side of the mountain track. Conditions for reaching the opening in the tower were as good as they were going to get. There was a window of fine weather before the storms closed in again. He followed the winding road, watching it curve upwards towards the menacing jumble of the castle.

'Are you ready?' asked Laura.

Phoenix shook his head slowly. Doubts were clawing at him. 'I could tell you better if I had any idea what's waiting for me up there.' He looked round at her. 'What if he's too strong? What if I don't know what to do?' And somewhere, from far away, came the secret voice.

You must. You must know what to do. He felt a light breeze skipping over the blanket of glistening snow. *It is your destiny.*

'What did you say?' Laura asked.

Phoenix started. Her words stabbed into his mind. He had been in a trance, repeating the words in his head. 'A voice,' he said. 'I hear a voice.' He tapped his forehead. 'It's in here. That instinct of mine, I know where it's coming from. I suppose I always did.'

Laura frowned. 'I don't understand.'

'It's Andreas. He's our guide.'

'Andreas! But he's . . .'

'Dead? Yes, I know. But he's speaking to me. The Vampyr can rise again, why not a mortal man?'

Foxton listened to their conversation for a while, then leaned forward. 'You really believe you are being guided by a spirit?'

'No,' Phoenix retorted. 'Andreas is inside me. I am meant to complete his destiny. It isn't a matter of believing. I *know*.'

Foxton met his eyes. 'I admire the certainty of youth. Now you have the chance to put your theory to the test. We're there.' He offered each of them a hand. 'Let me wish you well, young friends. If Robert is right about the room, then we shall not meet again. Good luck.'

Phoenix and Laura shook hands and climbed down from the carriage. The Szekelys had laid most of the explosive and were now clearing the snow from the squares and courtyards around the castle buildings. Bradshaw greeted Phoenix with a smile:

'We've been waiting for you. We have planned your way in. I hope you have a head for heights.' Phoenix lifted his gaze towards the roof of the tower. There was a trembling in his stomach and an unsteadiness about his legs. 'We're going to lower you from the topmost window.'

Phoenix heard Laura suck in her breath. 'And I've got to be lowered down the same way?'

Bradshaw gave another mischievous grin. 'If you want to go home, and your route truly lies in that room, then I'm afraid it's the only way.'

Phoenix could almost feel the fear eddying from her, reinforcing his own. 'Bird's Eye, you're sure we will find the gateway up there?'

Bird's Eye nodded. 'That's what I've seen. You and Laura standing before the gate.'

Phoenix sensed the truth of the image and set his jaw. 'Then up we go.'

What had appeared a frightening and dizzying prospect from below looked utterly terrifying from the heights of the tower. Dimitrescu's men had torn out the window in the top room and hammered away several stone blocks, leaving a large opening. Still as the day had appeared at ground level, at the summit of the tower a gale was blowing. Phoenix inspected the impromptu pulley system.

'You're sure this is safe?'

'As safe as we can make it,' Bradshaw replied. Phoenix's breath shuddered through him. 'Sorry I can't be more reassuring, lad.'

'Don't worry,' said Phoenix, fighting down his fears. 'I'm ready.' With that, he stepped into the makeshift harness and took a few tentative steps towards the opening. As he looked down his senses reeled. The whole earth seemed to pitch and sway beneath him. 'I'm not sure I can do this,' he stammered, the icy wind cutting into him.

'You have to,' said Ann, 'if you want to go home.' Then Phoenix could see the whole picture, the Vampyr-hunters ringing the castle, the explosives primed and ready, the gateway waiting just below his feet.

'You're right,' he said, his voice shaking. 'Lower me down.'

Bradshaw rested a hand on his shoulder. 'Once you're in line with the opening, you have to swing out to take you inside. Tug twice on the rope when you're out of the harness.'

Phoenix nodded, and confided in those nearest him: 'I can't swallow.'

Bradshaw smiled sympathetically. 'Just think what's at stake. It will carry you through.'

Phoenix looked around, at Bradshaw and Dimitrescu, Ann and Robert Van Helsing. 'How will you know if we've made it through the gate?'

'When we lower Laura down after you,' said Bradshaw, 'Hang on to the rope. Three tugs will mean you have opened the gate. Then we will set about burning this hideous place to the ground.'

The time was past for farewells, or for doubts. Gripping the rope for all he was worth, squeezing it until his knuckles went white, Phoenix stepped into the buffeting gale. As the Szekelys took the strain, he felt himself being lowered in sickening, jerking stages. The Szekelys had done what they could to give him some control over his progress. The rope ran underneath his thighs and he was able to steady himself by placing a foot in a loop at the bottom. Nothing however could prevent him swinging wildly in the swirling wind. And, no matter how he tried not to look down, nothing could stop the world below from spinning and lurching as he turned.

I really can't do this. Get me out of here. Take me back up! He was pleading inside, desperate to be hauled back to safety. He looked up. They wouldn't hear him in this wind, but he only had to tug on the rope to abandon his mission. He clung to the rope, feeling the rough fibres digging into his palms and fingers.

Please. But the descent continued until he was facing the opening. The snow had begun again, thickening and stinging his eyes. It was impossible to see what was inside. Expectation started to wear away the fright.

I'm almost there. Jut got to swing out. But the very idea of adding to the swaying movement of the rope tortured his insides. He hung there miserably, refusing to give up, but lacking the courage to go on.

What now?

Then he had his answer. The opening was gaping in front of him. It was now or never. Closing his eyes, Phoenix swung himself out. Three times he clawed at the stonework, finger-nails splintering, and three times he was torn away. But the fourth time he secured a handhold and dragged himself inside. As he disentangled himself from the harness, his eyes widened in fright. There was no sign of the gateway, but there was a familiar and terrifying object. In the far corner of the bare room, on a bed of filthy straw lay a roughly constructed box, some seven feet long. It didn't resemble the smooth, elaborately fashioned sarcophagus of popular imagination, but there was no disguising its purpose.

It was a coffin.

16

Unaware of Phoenix's discovery in the room below, Laura stepped into space with a frightened yelp.

'You'll be fine,' Bradshaw reassured her. 'Just don't . . .'

'Look down,' panted Laura, completing his sentence. 'Yes, I know.' So there she hung, just for a moment, squinting at her comrades through the driving snow. She smiled thinly, not knowing if they could see her face through the dizzy white maelstrom. 'I'm ready,' she shouted against the roar of the wind. 'Lower away.' And lower they did, the rope grinding and creaking disconcertingly above her head. 'At least I can't see the ground,' she said to herself through chattering teeth.

It was true. When she did dare to glance down she could see little but her own feet kicking helplessly against the chill air, keen to feel something solid beneath her. Then she could see it, the large, gashed opening in the side of the tower.

'Phoenix?' There was no reply, but what did she expect through the hollering wind? For a moment, the briefest of moments, she thought she saw movement. Curiously, it looked like two shadowy figures circling each other, but how could that be? 'This is it, Laura girl,' she told herself. 'Swing out.' But as she started to thrust her feet forward and her body back, she felt a hard tug on the rope. Thrown into a spin by its force, she looked up through the blizzard. Something was wrong.

'What is it? What's the matter?' She could just make out Bradshaw's face peering down at her. His mouth was open wide, his eyes staring. He was shouting something. A warning.

Clinging to the rope with one hand, Laura cupped the other theatrically to her ear. 'I can't hear you.' Then, straining hard, she started to make out snatches of what he was saying.

'Bird's Eye . . . the sight . . .'

She shook her head, and Bradshaw shouted louder.

'Someone in there . . . not safe.' Then the shouted plea: 'Come back up!' The two circling figures. The shadowy combat. It hadn't been an illusion. Somebody was in there with Phoenix. It was him. It had to be.

Dracul.

Feeling the upward movement of the rope, Laura screamed in protest. 'No. NO!'

Then, for all her fear of falling, she began to twist and turn, struggling for all she was worth against the direction of the rope. 'Please, you can't make me come back.' She glimpsed the puzzled look on Bradshaw's face. 'I have to be with him.'

'No,' he bawled back. 'It's a trap.'

'Please!'

Then she was hauling herself up out of the harness. 'I'll jump.'

'Don't be stupid, girl.'

'I will. I'm going home. I'd rather die than stay here.' That did the trick. Bradshaw gave a nod of resignation and she sat back down in the harness.

I'm coming, Phoenix.

She swung herself several times, twice cannoning into the stone wall, but eventually she found herself standing precariously on the edge of the opening. She was standing on the border between two worlds, the fading light of day behind her, the gloom of the mysterious chamber ahead. What she saw next filled her with despair. Phoenix was lying sprawled against the far wall. Blood was spilling from his mouth and nose. Between the fallen boy and Laura stood the figure from the portrait.

Dracul.

Laura eased herself out of the harness, careful not to make any more noise than was necessary. Meanwhile, Dracul advanced on Phoenix. Laura slipped her crossbow off her back, then looked around for the Angel. Phoenix's weapon lay smashed to smithereens by the coffin. She gulped, but her throat was dry and painful. That's when Phoenix saw her. He tried to control his expression, but hope registered in the widening of his eyes. Dracul turned.

'Welcome,' he said, speaking for the first time.

Laura pointed the bow at his heart, and released the trigger. The bleached face of Dracul registered contempt. He caught the quarrel in his taloned hand.

'Is that all you can do, child? I expected better.'

Laura felt icy fingers closing round her heart. In desperate fury, she lashed out with her crossbow. Strangely, Dracul snarled but he didn't retaliate. Then she understood. She was standing in a pool of watery winter sunlight at the entrance to the chamber.

'Phoenix, get him into the light.'

Dracul spun round, but Phoenix was already up. Armed with a mallet and steel pin, he hammered the spike into Dracul's shoulder, only prevented from penetrating the heart by a sweep of the creature's arm.

Csss! Dracul reeled, taking a step backwards towards the light before steadying himself and slashing with his talons.

'Hurt, does it?' asked Phoenix. 'Then try this.' He tried to hammer in a second pin, but the Vampyr was too quick, sending the mallet spinning from his hand. His reflexes were too fast for Laura too. In spite of the wound to his shoulder, he parried a second bolt.

'Your efforts are useless,' he snarled. He loomed over the boy, mouth widening to reveal his dripping fangs. But Phoenix wasn't finished yet. He scrabbled among the splintered wreckage of the Angel and yanked loose the steel bowstring. Just as Dracul was reaching to stop him, Laura swung her bow and cracked him across the skull.

'It will take more than that to stop the Lord of the Vampyrs,' sneered Dracul.

What it took was Phoenix. Hurling himself at the distracted Vampyr, he wrapped the wire round the creature's throat.

Css! Dracul reacted wildly, twisting and writhing as the makeshift noose bit into his cold flesh. The wild squirming pulled Phoenix off his feet. Twice he was dashed into the stone walls, the impact shuddering right through him. His hands were streaming with blood where the steel bowstring had bitten into his palms. But still he hung on.

'Don't let go!' Laura yelled, arming her crossbow a third time.

This time Dracul was unable to fend off the bolt and it crunched into his chest. Black blood spilled foaming from his mouth.

'Get out of the way,' Phoenix roared, releasing the wire. Laura did as she was told and Phoenix hurled himself at the staggering Vampyr, propelling him forward towards the opening. The moment the creature stumbled into the light, he started to scream. Phoenix was about to finish his grim task by hammering his hatchet between Dracul's shoulder blades, when he saw that there was no need. The last rays of the sun did their work. Flames leapt around him and started eating at his body, searing through to the bone. The white skin flaked away, peeling back from skull and skeleton, then from deep inside the disintegrating Vampyr came a death-shriek that echoed hellishly into the gathering dusk. In just a few instants Dracul had crumbled to dust.

17

'Is that it?' Laura asked, her face flushed. 'Have we won?'

'No,' said a voice behind her. 'You haven't.'

The speaker was Adams. He was standing in the doorway, his large frame set against the dimming winter light.

'Tell her, Phoenix,' he said. 'Explain that our fanged friend was expendable. He was a puppet, no more.' Adams glanced in mock sadness at the pile of dust on the floor.

'Did you really think it would be this easy, Laura? You can stake a Vampyr, but how do you destroy my master? What is he: a haunting, a phantom, a spirit who roams the world? You are trying to kill a vapour.'

Laura looked at Phoenix.

'That's not the whole truth though, is it Adams?' Phoenix retorted. 'He is not a spirit by choice, is he? Why else would he fight so hard and so long to enter our world?' He saw Adams' expression change and knew he was on the right track. 'In some way I don't yet understand the Gamesmaster suffered a defeat. He became a ghost, or something like. Well Adams, how am I doing?'

Adams snorted. 'It's true. My master longs to be free, to take on physical form. Believe me, when he does, he will choose a perfect vehicle for his power. Sadly, you will not be there to witness it.' He looked around the chamber. 'So this is your goal,' he said. 'The room with an exit and no entrance.' He shook his head. 'Did you really trust Bird's Eye? Bird Brain is more like it.'

'But the gateway . . .' said Laura.

'Gateway,' sneered Adams. 'Do you see any gateway? All is illusion. This room is a dead-end street, the final cul-de-sac.'

Laura snapped a bolt into the groove of her crossbow. 'There *is* a gateway,' she said. 'There has to be.' She pointed the bow at Adams' heart.

'Oh, put it down,' said Adams. 'You won't shoot.'

'Don't push me,' said Laura.

But Adams did just that. Stretching out an arm, he pushed her shoulder, shoving her back towards the opening. 'I know you Laura. I know the softness inside you, the weakness. When you look at me, all you can see is the boy I was. Why kid yourself? You can't kill.'

'Stop it!' She gripped the stock of the crossbow. 'Get back.'

Phoenix leapt at Adams but was hurled across the room, crashing painfully into the far wall.

'And if I don't?' asked Adams, shoving her again.

'I'll shoot.'

'No,' said Adams reaching for her again. 'No, you won't.'

'I will,' she tried, her finger squeezing the trigger.

'And cut me down in cold blood. I don't think so.' Then he pushed her again, right to the edge of the opening. Laura's feet scrambled on the stone floor. A split second later she lost her footing and tumbled backwards.

'No!'

Phoenix picked himself up, and launched himself forward. He made a despairing lunge for Laura, but he was too late. Or so he thought. Just as Laura was falling backwards, a blurred figure hit her from behind, blasting the breath from her body and jettisoning her forward across the room. As she sprawled on the straw-covered floor, Laura felt the crossbow go spinning from her hands.

'Dimitrescu!'

The Szekely leader used the rope to continue his forward momentum. Having swept Laura to safety he twisted round and threw himself at Adams.

172

'Your contagion dies here, broodmaster,' he yelled, clinging to Adams.

But Adams wasn't to be overcome so easily. Crashing his elbows into Dimitrescu's ribs, he smashed his fist into the Vampyr-hunter's body, propelling him back out into the storm where the Szekely fighter hung winded and one-handed, spinning helplessly on the end of the rope.

'Nikolai!'

'Save your breath,' snarled Adams. 'Within the hour night will have fallen. The dark angels will flaunt the skies and you will all be dead.' He stroked Laura's cheek. 'Or maybe I will have them turn you into a pretty little attraction for the undead. Ever wondered how you'd look with fangs?'

Laura recoiled at his touch. Out of the corner of her eye, she could see Dimitrescu still hanging, his legs pedalling as he hung precariously.

'Take your hands off her!' yelled Phoenix.

In reply, Adams slapped him to the floor. Laura ran to Phoenix and helped him up into a sitting position. Their backs were pressed against the wall, their eyes searching frantically for a way out, the way out Bird's Eye had promised them. But there was no escape.

Adams came on, framed against the storm. Behind him, Dimitrescu was straining to hang on, his muscles screaming. Adams' talons, his fangs, his dark eyes flashed, his leering face glistened in the dying light.

'Say your prayers, Legendeer. Cry out to whatever gods you believe in.' He was towering above them, death-fire in his eyes.

It was in that moment that Laura spotted her bow. She caught Phoenix's eye and saw the look of recognition. He knew what he had to do. Instantly he threw himself on Adams and Laura dived for the bow. Adams shook Phoenix off with ease and lunged with such heart-stopping speed that Laura's bolt was touching his body by the time she had it in her hand. This time there was no hesitation. She shot the quarrel. Adams

173

fell back, squirming and writhing on the bolt, a savage shriek bursting from his throat. But, while Laura fumbled with the second bolt, Adams was already starting to draw out the first.

'Hurry it up, will you!' Phoenix cried, still wracked with pain from Adams' attacks. He could see his nemesis easing the point of the bolt from his punctured flesh.

'I'm trying!'

Then the bolt was in the groove. Leaning back, Laura took aim. But there was no respite. Adams was still coming, his taloned hand slashing at her face and throat. Phoenix was swinging desperately with the hatchet he had drawn from his belt, barely fending off the frenzied attack.

'Reload. Reload!' He saw Adams' fangs dripping venom over his face. 'Please!'

But Adams was too fast, too powerful. He dashed the crossbow from Laura's hand. Phoenix closed his eyes. All hope gone, he awaited the death-blow.

18

The death-blow never came. A new struggle had exploded about him.

'Nikolai!'

Dimitrescu must have succeeded in steadying himself and now had his arms and legs wrapped round the astonished Adams. Hauling Adams away from the two teenagers, Dimitrescu threw the pair of them back out into the storm. In an instant they were clinging together, high above the ground. They were like condemned twins, dancing from the gallows.

'We've got to do something,' screamed Laura, searching for the crossbow.

Phoenix reached the weapon first. He snatched it up and raced to the opening. 'It's no good,' he groaned despairingly. 'I can't get a clear shot.'

The two figures were spinning ever more wildly, clinging to one another and wrestling for supremacy at the same time, becoming a single dark shape in the confusion of the storm, and the murky uncertainty of the growing dusk. Phoenix heard the sounds of the castle. The creaking, the rustling, the hissing. The Vampyr Legion was coming to life.

'Do something,' cried Laura. 'We've got to help Nikolai.'

Phoenix could hear the dark menace of the awakening ghouls. In a matter of minutes they would be swarming over the walls. He aimed the bow, but he didn't dare shoot. 'I can't. I could hit Nikolai.'

'Phoenix, you have to take a chance. Shoot.'

Phoenix stared at that threshing figures. He trained the crossbow on the twisting pair and felt despair like an ache gnawing at him. 'It's no good.' He closed his eyes and felt the tears coming. He heard the Szekely leader's cries of pain as Adams proved the more powerful. 'Nikolai, I'm so sorry.' That's when it came. A voice flooded his mind, like joy.

Do it. Phoenix eyes flickered.

No! Don't even open your eyes. Trust what you know within.

Instinct took over, and Phoenix shot. Then, as quickly as it started, it was over. There was a piercing cry and one of the fighters fell, arms flailing into the depths of the blizzard.

Laura turned round, her face flushed with joy: 'Phoenix, you did it. Nikolai is all right.' Then her voice changed. 'We have to open the gate. It's almost dark. They're going to blow the castle before the Vampyrs can rise.'

Phoenix nodded. At last he knew what to do. For a moment he watched Dimitrescu climbing up the rope, then turned to the wall. He placed the tips of his fingers against the stone-work.

Trust yourself, came the silent speaker. *The gateway is where you wish it to be.* There they were, the numbers from the computer game, the silver and golden numerals that had flashed in the portal of light. **333 666 999.**

Do as before. Feel with your mind. He saw the numbers glowing in the darkness. *Guide me, Andreas. Show me.*

He pressed his fingers into the stone, gouged them in, and suddenly something was happening. The ungiving stone yielded, becoming molten and plastic. His fingers were moulding it, carving the gateway out of molten rock.

'Phoenix,' cried Laura, 'You've done it! We're going home.' Outside, the storm was beginning to abate and the moon was drifting lazily from behind the clouds. 'It's time,' said Laura. 'The charges are laid.'

Phoenix nodded. 'The Vampyr perishes this night,' he said. 'Let's go.'

'Listen,' said Laura as they approached the gate. The first

explosions were ripping through the castle's great hall. 'We did it.'

Without another word, they stepped together through the gate.

Victorious.

EPILOGUE

Make or Break

It is the way of life that after 'The End' there is always something else.

Christmas came and went that year. *Vampyr Legion* duly appeared and topped the computer games sales chart on both sides of the Atlantic. But it was what didn't happen that mattered to Phoenix and Laura.

The Parallel Reality suit didn't materialize. The game's players didn't *get into* that game in any physical sense. The gateway between the worlds didn't open. The Gamesmaster didn't appear.

It was the end.

Or was it? Day after day, Phoenix found himself asking the same question. What if there was something *after* the end?

'Seen this?' Laura asked on the bus into school.

Phoenix took the label from her, saw the miniature photograph printed on it, and gasped. 'Where did you get it?'

'It was on a milk carton in the supermarket.'

Phoenix stared at the photograph. It was Adams, but not as they had seen him in the myth-world. This was Adams as he had been once upon a time in another life, a human being with at least a suspicion 'of innocence, a smiling schoolboy. Before *The Legendeer*. Before the darkness.

'Hard to believe he was ever like that, isn't it?' asked Laura.
'I know.'

Phoenix read the appeal:

Missing
Can you help?

Steven Adams is fourteen and has been missing for four months. He vanished from his home without warning and hasn't been seen since. He is dark-haired, of slim build and tall for his age.

There were more physical details and finally a number to call.

'I can't believe it's the same person,' said Laura.

'He is in a different world,' said Phoenix, 'and living by different laws.'

'You think he survived the fall, then?'

'I *know* he did.'

'How?'

'He flew up to the chamber, didn't he? He could also fly down again. Besides, I have this feeling.'

'You almost sound as if you want him to be alive.'

You don't know how much. 'Maybe I do.'

Laura stared at him in disbelief. 'But how could you? He's insane. He almost killed us both.'

Phoenix looked out of the window of the bus. 'But when he's alive, I'm alive.' Laura's shocked expression demanded an explanation.

'You mustn't ever tell my parents,' said Phoenix, 'But I don't feel as if I belong here any more. Everything is so small, so trivial, so tedious. I am the Legendeer. My destiny is out there with the demons. I belong to the myth-world. They are the dark half of me.'

'That's crazy talk.'

'Is it?' said Phoenix. 'Is it really? Why?'

'It just is.'

'Listen,' Phoenix told her. 'Ever since I returned I've been desperate to go back.'

'To Csespa?'

'No, it's all over there. I need to be wherever the Games-master is.'

'Is something wrong at home?' asked Laura. 'Are your parents giving you a hard time?'

'Far from it,' said Phoenix, 'They could have been a lot worse. They're actually letting me out again by myself, as long as I take my keep-in-touch kit with me.' He held up a bleeper and a mobile phone.

'Don't believe in half-measures, do they?' said Laura.

'No, but it isn't them anyway. It's me. Remember the entry I read you from Andreas' diary? The way he felt like a stranger in his own world. That's me too. It's the way it's always been, I suppose.'

'But look what happened to him!'

'Oh, I know exactly what happened to him. It didn't mean he was wrong though, did it? It isn't over, Laura, I know that. In your heart of hearts, I think you do too.'

Laura nudged Phoenix. 'It's our stop.' Phoenix followed her off the bus. He knew she was glad of a break from that particular conversation. But there was no respite, not from *The Legendeer*.

'Have you played it yet?' asked a first year in front of them.

'*Vampyr Legion*?' said his friend. 'Yes, it's cool.'

'Could have been better though, couldn't it? They were supposed to have those Parallel Reality suits. That was a let-down.'

'There'll be no let-down this time.' Phoenix and Laura exchanged glances.

'How do you mean?'

'It's in here.' He produced a copy of *Gamestation* magazine.

'Could I see that?' asked Phoenix, looking over the boy's shoulder.

'Get your own.'

'I will. I mean, I have. I've got a subscription. It'll be on the mat when I get home.' He saw the hesitation in the boy's face. 'Look, I'm not going to steal it. Here, you can even keep hold of it while I read.' The boy agreed and Phoenix and Laura read the piece that headlined the news section:

Make or break-time for Magna-com

It is make or break time for Magna-com's highly-successful *Legendeer* series. Despite more than healthy sales figures this autumn and winter, the company's flagship game will be judged ultimately on its promise to come up with a: 'feel-around, fear-around experience'. That means delivery of the long-awaited Parallel Reality suit that will transform computer games from something you watch to something you take part in. A third failure to deliver the technology would be sure to disappoint the series' millions of fans. And disappointed fans quite simply stop buying. *The Legendeer, Part Three* is currently under development.

Word has it, the game's designers are planning a final, conclusive battle between good and evil.

Let's hope Magna-com don't come out of it as big-time losers.

'Thanks,' said Phoenix, walking away.

'That's it then,' said Laura, hurrying after him. 'You've got your way.'

Phoenix met her eyes. 'It doesn't matter what I want,' he told her. 'It's what has to be. This is my destiny, just as it was Andreas'.'

At that very moment, in John Graves' study, destiny was on somebody else's mind. The as-yet undeciphered sequence of numbers was flashing across the computer screen. It was the voice of the Gamesmaster:

Have you read it, Legendeer? Such perceptive work. **Make or break** *it is.*

But believe me, young hero, it is not I who will be broken on the wheel of Fate. Your victories have been won over my disciples,

181

not over me. I have had to watch while they failed me. Soon I will pay you and all your kind back in blood and terror. My strength is growing. I have planted a seed, and it is growing sturdy and tall. Soon I will have no need of others to do my bidding. I will tread the stars again, and burn out your senses with my fury. Enjoy your victory while it lasts, boy.

For the first time in so long, I can smell the rising wind, I can feel the beat of my blood, the buzzing of my nerves, the snaking tug of my muscles. I can hear the groaning of the worlds, the miserable pleading of my enemies. I can smell their funeral pyres. There is no peace for you, young hero. You are about to reap the whirlwind.

The game is not over until it is won, Legendeer.

Game on.

Also by Alan Gibbons

Shadow of the Minotaur

'Real life' or the death-defying adventures of the Greek myths, with their heroes and monsters, daring deeds and narrow escapes – which would you choose?

For Phoenix it's easy. He hates his new home and the new school where he is bullied. He's embarrassed by his computer geek dad. But when he logs on to *The Legendeer*, the game his dad is working on, he can be a hero. He is Theseus fighting the terrifying Minotaur, or Perseus battling with snake-haired Medusa.

The trouble is, *The Legendeer* is more than just a game. Play it if you dare.

Warriors of the Raven

The game opens up the gateway between our world and the world of the myths.

The Gamesmaster almost has our world at his mercy. Twice before fourteen-year-old Phoenix has battled against him in *Shadow of the Minotaur* and *Vampyr Legion*, but Warriors of the Raven is the game at its most complex and deadly level. This time, Phoenix enters the arena for the final conflict, set in the world of Norse myth. Join Phoenix in Asgard to fight Loki, the Mischief-maker, the terrifying Valkyries, dragons and fire demons – and hope for victory. Our future depends on him.

Also by Alan Gibbons

The Defender

When Kenny Kincaid turns his back on the past he has no idea of the legacy he is bequeathing his only son, Ian.

Was he escaping from the paramilitaries, from too much violence and bloodshed, too many victims? Or was he betraying the Cause, turning his back on his comrades-in-arms when he fled clutching his baby son and a quarter of a million pounds from a bank job? They think so, and they're intent on revenge. Years later Kenny is still a target – and now so is Ian.

Father and son are going to have to live with it . . . or die with it.

Controversial, compulsive reading, this is an unputdownable thriller.

'A powerful thriller . . . Many layers, no simplifications.'
Irish Times

'Gibbons makes you feel what it is like when everyday life goes haywire. There is lots of action, and 14-year-old Ian is easy to relate to.' *Guardian*

Alan Gibbons

Caught in the Crossfire

'You know what happens to people like you? You get hit in the crossfire.'

Shockwaves sweep the world in the aftermath of 11 September. The Patriotic League barely need an excuse in their fight to get Britain back for the British, but this is chillingly perfect.

Rabia and Tahir are British Muslims, Daz and Jason are out looking for trouble, Mike and Liam are brothers on different sides. None of them will escape unscarred from the terrifying and tragic events which will weave their lives together.

Marking a new dimension in his writing on race, riots and real life *Caught in the Crossfire* is an unforgettable novel that Alan Gibbons needed to write.

'Gibbons' writing often addresses worrying issues of social justice but never as powerfully as in this novel . . . the writing – the short, sharp pieces that take us into the mind of each character – is accessible and compulsive.'
Wendy Cooling, *The Bookseller*

Alan Gibbons

The Edge

Danny is a boy on the edge. A boy teetering on the brink of no return, living in fear.

Cathy is his mother. She's been broken by fear.

Chris Kane is fear – and they belong to him.

But one day they escape. They're looking for freedom, for the promised land where they can start really living. Instead they find prejudice, and danger of another kind.

Uncompromising and disturbing, but utterly readable, Alan Gibbons' latest novel positively crackles with tension as he writes about a mother and her son desperate to start a new life.

'This is a fast and compelling "must read" that is disturbing in ways that are bound to make teenagers confront important issues like racism and endemic violence. I can't recommend it highly enough.'
Books for Keeps